Save a Vamp, Take a Crown

Flawed Fates

Book Two

Cover artwork by Alex Calder

www.addictivecovers.com

Interior artwork by Cauldron Press

www.cauldronpress.ca

A huge thank you to-

Allison Woerner and Tamara Bui for Alpha Reading

Maxine Meyer for Copy Editing.

Imogen Evans for Proofreading & Editing.

SAVE A Vamp
TAKE A Crown

INTERNATIONAL BESTSELLING AUTHOR
SEDONA ASHE WRITING AS

DARCI R. ACULA

This is not a reverse harem. There is only one fated mate, and he's a vampire who's so hot, you'll want to lick him!
This book features an obsessed, delusional, and violent stalker who will do whatever it takes to get Journee (the FMC). There are scenes in this book that are a bit darker than my normal writing style... people get injured and killed.
There is no bullying or abuse from her soulmate. Even though other women are vying for the MC's attention, he only has eyes for Journee and is quick to shut all other females down. The vampire prince has a monstrous vampiric form with some fun attachments (hee hee), that he's eager to use to protect and satisfy his soulmate.

CONTENTS

RECAP

zyon

I laughed at the wide-eyed terror on Journee's beautiful face. She'd passed out cold before I could reassure her that I was only teasing—I'd never actually ask her to take both of them.

It was a challenge to fit my huge shifter body on the bed, but I finally managed to curl myself around my sleeping soulmate. A sense of calm settled over me as I watched the steady rise and fall of her chest. I brushed a finger through her dark hair and listened to her heartbeat as it settled into a slow, steady rhythm.

My muscles relaxed and relief welled up in me, with pride following close on its heels. Journee was tougher than she looked. She hadn't run screaming into the night after seeing my exaggerated features or monstrous size. Well, she'd been screaming, but she hadn't been running.

I hadn't believed there was a human on earth who'd be able to stand in front of my vampiric form without passing out from fear. After all, how often did you come face to face with a monster standing nine feet tall? And if my size wasn't enough to terrify humans, my appearance would definitely finish the job. I looked like the twisted love-child of a demon and a gargoyle.

After I'd first shifted into this creature, I'd spent the next century trying to figure out why my vampiric shift was so different from other vampires. It hadn't been easy, but I'd found a dusty book in the back of a crumbling bookshop that referenced an old scroll bearing a prophecy about a monster like me being born. That is when I found out I was called the 'Abomination.'

Unwilling to accept that answer, I'd spent the next century trying to disprove it. But most of the documents regarding the prophecy had been hidden by the Hunters, and who knew if they even still existed? It wasn't like I could walk up to one again and ask. I'd tried that, and it didn't end well.

Hunters preferred to kill rather than chat over coffee. Their DNA was hardwired to track and kill vampires. Just like vampires were driven to drink blood to survive, Hunters were driven to seek the thrill of killing vampires. They'd done well to hide their serial killer vibes from the humans by claiming to be protectors of the weaker species. But I suspected that if they'd ever managed to kill all the vampires, their bloodlust would've driven them to pick a new species to target.

Journee shivered. Unable to get the blanket out from beneath my mate without disturbing her, I rested my wing over her body and tucked her closer against me. My natural form might be cool as ice, but this form radiated heat.

Journee's soft sigh of contentment had my body trembling. How could she accept me this quickly? It was only recently that I'd accepted what I was and had made the decision to keep the monster inside me hidden from the rest of the world. Here she was, so trusting in me that she fell asleep in my arms.

My wing ached in protest at being stretched, and I felt the burned edges of the gash reopen, but I ignored the discomfort. Abner's whip had cracked across the thick leathery skin, slashing far deeper than I'd thought and scorching a wide swath of skin. Each time I moved, searing pain would spread through my wing and into my shoulder.

I could have healed the injury, but that would've used more of my waning energy reserves, which would force me to feed. There was no way I was leaving Journee's side, nor would I reduce her to being a feeder, so feeding would have to wait. Besides, even if I were willing to leave her, I couldn't be seen in this form roaming around the castle. It didn't matter. The injury would heal on its own by morning, and I could ignore the pain until then.

With my Irenvyth tucked in the safety of my arms, I closed my eyes and focused on her soft orange and vanilla scent, allowing it to ease the agitation, guilt and rage that pumped through my veins. Until I calmed myself, I wasn't going to be able to shift back.

Cradling her to my chest, I silently vowed to protect her. I would shield her from as much physical and emotional pain as I could for the rest of her life. She was mine to treasure. That last thought had my body aching with the need to claim her all over again until I had memorized every inch of her stunning body.

But while I could go all night, Journee couldn't take another round with my monster. I wasn't complaining about her need to rest. She'd given me a gift I'd never thought possible. Having sex in my vampiric form was something I'd never expected to experience, and it had been mind-blowing beyond anything I could have imagined.

On the rare occasions I'd shifted into this form in the past, I'd spent the entire time fighting to shift back to my natural form. Tonight, I'd enjoyed my vampiric form, something I'd never done before. Discovering I could use it to please my soulmate was thrilling. While I was eager to savor Journee's body in my natural form, I couldn't help but wonder if it would be as intense as it was in this form. I hoped my mate would be interested in bonding in both of my forms.

For the first time in my long life, I found myself eager to spend more time in my vampiric form, but only in the safety of my chambers with Journee. I felt content... and almost comfortable.

I would never be able to sleep if I continued down this train of thought, so I forced my tense muscles to relax into the soft mattress. To my surprise, I drifted to sleep within minutes.

CHAPTER
1

zyon

C losing my eyes, I focused on my mate's heartbeat and hoped it would calm my monster. If I were lucky, it would help me shift back sooner rather than later.

Five seconds passed, then ten seconds, and finally thirty seconds. My eyes snapped open.

Something wasn't right.

Tilting my head to the side, my eyebrows drew together as I stared down at my sleeping mate. Her beautiful skin was still bare from our bonding, and I pulled the sheet over her as I carefully counted each soft beat of her heart.

An icy tendril of fear began to weave through me. Her heart was beating far slower than that of a typical human at rest.

Although, perhaps this was her natural resting heart rate? Yes, I was simply overreacting. Humans weren't all the same, so surely their resting heart rates could vary wildly, right?

Thump.

Thump… thump.

With each beat, her heart slowed more. Or was I imagining things due to the fresh bond between us?

"Journee? Wake up, love." Pushing myself into a sitting position, I gathered her into my arms, giving her a gentle shake.

There were dark purple circles beneath her eyes, and her skin was pale from stress and fatigue. My stomach twisted with guilt for waking her, but I needed to know she was okay.

Thud…

I waited to hear her heartbeat again, my own heart ceasing to beat while I listened. There was only silence.

"Journee!" Raw terror like nothing I'd felt in my life tore through my body and mind like a rabid tiger seeking to destroy everything in its path.

Dropping her limp body onto the disheveled comforter, I quickly straddled her unresponsive form. She nearly disappeared beneath me, and my throat tightened at the reminder of how small my mate was in comparison to my monstrous size.

My soul had desperately needed to brush against her soul, and like a selfish beast, I'd given in to the desire.

I'd allowed myself to take what I craved and claim her as mine. But it had pushed Journee's body too far, and now I'd lost her. And it was all my fault.

Her chest relaxed, no longer moving. Journee had stopped breathing.

A roar tore from my throat. "Breathe! Don't you dare leave me!"

I began chest compressions, trying my best to remember how to resuscitate a human. The human governments had pressed the issue, claiming vampires needed to know basic CPR in case we accidentally took feeding too far and needed to save someone. Why hadn't I paid more attention during the required classes?

Oh yes, because I'd never cared if a human died. There were far too many of them stinking up the planet as it was. Plus, I'd known there wasn't a chance I'd place my mouth on a filthy human to breathe air into their lungs.

Not a chance in hell.

But things had changed. I cared about a human—more than I'd ever cared about anything in my life. But I didn't know how to save her because I'd been a self-absorbed vampire who hadn't wished to be bothered by those he deemed beneath him.

And now, my arrogance might cost me my Irenvyth.

"Journee!" I bellowed, but again, there was no response.

Through blurred vision, I continued my clumsy, ineffective efforts to bring her back. "I need you. Please don't leave me."

Just when I had given up hope, there was the faintest of sounds from her chest. I stilled, tilting my head to hear better.

Thump.

My heart lurched hard enough to pull a muscle at that single, soft beat from her heart.

Thump.

Thump. Thump. Thump.

With each beat, her heart grew louder, until it was as strong as it had been before our bonding—or maybe even stronger?

How curious.

I studied my female intently. I'd been so sure her heart had given out, and she'd died, but mere minutes later, her heart was beating like that of an Olympic athlete. Maybe I'd misjudged humans, and they weren't all terribly dull. Mine was certainly proving to be anything but boring.

Which she confirmed when her eyelids flew open and her glowing gray eyes locked onto me. Wait, *glowing?*

The bedroom was pitch black, so her eyes couldn't be reflecting the glow of a light or the fire. Perhaps they were reflecting the glow from my eyes? Yes, that had to be it. I leaned toward her, wanting a closer look.

"Curiouser and curiouser—" My words were cut off when Journee brought her knee up between my legs. Hard.

Grunting in shock, I toppled over. Even with pain clouding my brain, I remembered to roll to the side, trying to keep from burying her under my full weight.

I shouldn't have worried.

Journee moved fast. By the time my body impacted with the bed, she'd slipped out from beneath me, and her weight shoved me down into the pillowy mattress.

Struggling to comprehend how she'd moved faster than I could track, I finally blamed it on being distracted, thanks to the excruciating pain radiating through my nether regions.

Journee's legs locked around my waist. The petal-soft skin of her arm brushed against me as she snaked her arm around my neck.

Like a python coiling around its prey, she slowly tightened her hold, cutting into my windpipe. Dragging a hand away from my crotch, I wrapped my fingers around her wrist.

"Journee? It's okay. It's me, Zyon. You stopped breathing, and I had to resuscitate you."

I tried to pull her arm away from my neck, but she proved to be surprisingly strong for a human. Not wanting to roll over and squish her, I shoved to my feet.

My sudden movement managed to dislodge my mate from my back, but it wasn't enough to startle her awake her from whatever dream she was acting out.

"Journee, wake up!" I croaked.

My gorgeous little soulmate leaped off the bed, flinging herself at me. With a shocking speed, she climbed my body to wrap her thighs around my neck until she was on my massive shoulders, like a toddler sitting on an adult's shoulders at a concert.

"Vamp," she breathed against my ear.

What was going on? Had she lost her mind? Did she think I'd been trying to kill her? Had that triggered her instinct to defend herself?

My heart shattered. I'd never hurt her—*could* never hurt her. She was mine, and just the thought of her believing for a single second that I'd injure her was enough to crush my soul.

Moving carefully so she didn't fall, I lowered us until I was sitting on the edge of the bed. Grabbing her thighs, I attempted to dislodge her gently. I'd been hoping to topple her off onto the mattress, where she'd be less likely to injure herself.

It turned out she was stuck to me as though her thighs had been super-glued around my neck. None of this made any sense. It shouldn't have been so difficult. I was a vampire, and she was human.

"Tumbleweed. It's okay." I kept my voice low and soothing. "You're safe. No one is going to hurt you. Abner's dead. Your stalker is gone."

Journee's only response was to flex her legs. She was beginning to cut off my blood flow, and I was growing slightly dizzy.

"Okay, enough. Are you even awake?" I couldn't help the small growl that slipped out.

Maybe she was sleepwalking? Or, more accurately, sleep-strangling?

I stood, my fingers tightening around her legs. My muscles strained as I tried once again to pry her legs off me while controlling my strength not to injure her.

"I don't think so. You're not getting away from me," Journee snarled.

Even though I was worried, I chuckled. "Babe, I know vampires aren't really your thing, but we are kind of together forever now. It's a done deal."

Journee yanked hard, pulling all her weight to the left. The unexpected move knocked me off balance, and we staggered into the wall. There was no question that if I used my full vampire strength, it would be easy to dislodge Journee from her perch on my shoulders. But I didn't see any way to do it without injuring her.

"Wake up, Journee!" I bellowed.

My mate responded by digging her nails deep into my bare shoulders.

"Argh!" My roar was more from shock than pain.

It took some doing, but I finally managed to topple her off my shoulders and onto the bed. My relief was short-lived.

No sooner had Journee's butt hit the velvet comforter than she'd snatched the sheet from the bed, and with a speed that would be impressive even for a vampire, she launched herself at me.

I should have dodged her, but my worry over my mate combined with my surprise slowed my reflexes. In an instant, Journee had the black sheet wrapped neatly around my neck and had climbed astride my shoulders. Again.

What. The. Frick.

This time, when her thighs squeezed, she simultaneously yanked at a slipknot in the sheet, effectively cutting off the blood flow to my brain.

It was at that moment Nathan chose to disobey my order.

A human wouldn't have been able to see in the dark room, but Nathan was a vampire with near-perfect night vision. I could see him as though the room were ablaze with light.

"Zyon? Journee? Are you okay?" Nathan's mask of worry immediately morphed into confusion, which was quickly followed by amusement.

Slapping a hand over his eyes, Nathan backed toward the door, knocking over a side table in the process.

"Oh man, I seriously did not need to know what you two do in your personal time. I mean... dang, bro! I had no idea you were into some kinky stuff."

"It's not what you think," I hissed, trying to wedge my fingers beneath the sheet tightening around my neck.

"Listen, there's no judgment from me, man! You do you." Nathan laughed, continuing to move toward the exit.

Journee stilled, the sheet around my neck going slack as her attention focused squarely on Nathan. With the grace of a gold-medal gymnast, she dismounted from my shoulders and rushed toward Nathan.

I was forced to use vampiric speed to catch her. Grabbing her around the waist, I pulled her up into my arms as though she were a runaway bride. I had to nearly crush Journee against my chest and curl my wings around us to keep her from escaping.

"Out!" I shouted the command, knowing at any moment she was likely to slip from my grasp again.

While I had limited experience with humans, I didn't think it should be this difficult to control one.

"I'm going. I'm going." Nathan slammed the door. His footsteps and laughter echoed as he moved down the hall.

I groaned, and it had nothing to do with the tiny vixen in my arms who'd just sunk her teeth into my chest. Nope.

It had everything to do with the teasing I'd have to deal with from Nathan. There was no way I would ever live this down. That man had a long memory and a lifetime to match it.

Journee squirmed in my hold, trying to wiggle free. She was stuck in one heck of a nightmare!

Deciding the gentle approach wasn't working with her, I switched tactics. If she wanted to play rough, we'd play rough.

Whirling around, I flung her on the bed. I sent Journee flying with enough force to knock the wind from her lungs but not enough to hurt her. The goal was to shock her out of this trance, not to injure her.

Using my mate's brief moment of stunned stillness to my advantage, I threw myself onto the bed. I pinned her lithe body beneath mine and gripped both her wrists in one of my much larger hands. Hauling Journee's arms above her head, I pressed them deep into the mattress.

Her legs wrapped around mine, although whether she was trying to attack me or escape me, I couldn't figure out.

With her body crushed beneath mine, I tried to rouse her from the dream's unrelenting hold.

"Tumbleweed, please wake up," I pleaded. "Love, I don't know what's going on, but I swear on my life you're safe. Come back to me."

Journee managed to wrap her legs around my waist, bucking wildly as she tried to push me away from her.

While my only concern was for her safety, other parts of my body couldn't help but sit up and take notice as she rocked against my hips.

My Irenvyth released an adorable growl through tightly clenched teeth.

The monster in me pushed for control, utterly convinced we could make her forget all about the dream. All I needed to do was give in and claim her body...

I groaned as Journee arched her back. She pressed her soft, bare breasts against my chest, further inciting the thing inside me.

My soulmate was having a horrible dream, but the beast only saw his mate presenting herself.

Seriously, this is not the time. With supreme effort, I held myself utterly still as her hips continued to rock against mine. I tried to ignore the way her orange-scented skin brushed against me.

Never in my life had I experienced such a primal urge to mate as I was fighting against at that moment.

Never in my long, long life had there been any woman who I craved as much as I did the raven-haired beauty beneath me.

Finally realizing she was pinned, Journee bared her teeth at me.

I recognized a threat when I saw one, but her display did nothing to douse the inferno of lust blazing inside me.

My vampiric instincts demanded I flash my fangs in return, ensuring she knew I wasn't intimidated by her. But my mate wasn't a vampire. She was a human who seemed to be caught in a terrifying dream that had her fighting for her life.

With effort, I resisted my vampiric instinct. Instead, I leaned forward and gave her a quick kiss on the mouth. I knew she might bite me, but I didn't really mind a bit of teeth in the bedroom.

Journee's body went stiff as a board.

Pulling my head back, I watched her eyes widen, and the fog dissipate from the depths of her eyes. The faraway look faded, and I watched as awareness returned.

"Zyon?" she whispered, her voice sleepy and her brow wrinkling in confusion. "What's going on?"

"You were dreaming, my love." Relief washed through me, and I pressed my lips to hers for a second kiss.

It was intended to be a sweet peck, but Journee deepened the kiss, and I couldn't pull away. I knew I needed to move and let her up. I needed to release her hands. But I couldn't find the strength because I found I enjoyed having her pinned helplessly beneath me.

And despite the fact she'd been acting out a dream, Journee's body had responded to mine. She moaned into my mouth, her legs tightening around my waist. Thanks to all her wild bucking against me, she'd grown slick with the evidence of her desire.

Taking a deep breath, I filled my lungs with the sweet fragrance of my Irenvyth's lust. "Journee."

I had to stop this now, or I'd be unable to resist claiming her body all over again.

Reluctantly, I loosened my grip around her wrists,

intending to free her arms. But Journee laced her fingers through mine, keeping our hands pressed to the mattress above her head.

"What happened to your chest?"

Glancing down, I found her gaze was locked on one of the bite wounds on my chest.

"Did I do that?" Journee's voice trembled. "Please, tell me I didn't do that."

CHAPTER 2

journee

"Did I do that?" My stomach twisted painfully as I looked at the angry bite marks on his skin. "Please, tell me I didn't do that."

Zyon's eyes lit up, and he puffed out his chest. "Yes, you did."

The insane vampire sounded proud, even as my cheeks burned in humiliation.

He lowered his head to nuzzle my neck. "And I liked it. Maybe you should do it again."

"I hurt you! We need to get you an antibiotic. Human bites are dangerous!" My protests turned to moans as Zyon rolled his hips, pressing his hard bulge against the apex of my thighs.

"How are you so adorable?" Zyon's husky chuckle left me panting. "I'm a vampire. Your bite is no more a danger to my health than a paper cut."

It had been an accident, but I'd still injured him. Lifting my head, I pressed a soft kiss to his injured skin. "I'm sorry."

My hands were still above my head, my fingers intertwined with his. Zyon pushed our clasped hands into the bed and peered down at me with glowing eyes. "I'm not. Stop worrying, Tumbleweed. I assure you, I've healed from injuries far worse than these."

The memory of the deep slash across his wing flashed into my mind, and I searched for the wound. It was still there and appeared not much better than it had the night before.

"Why aren't you healed?" I squirmed from his hold and moved to inspect the damage that Abner had done to my mate.

"Stop fussing, little mate." Zyon gently pulled his wing from between my hands. "By this afternoon, it will be healed."

"I thought vampires healed faster?" I chewed on my lip, trying to remember vampire anatomy class.

"I'll need to eat to heal more quickly." He refused to look at me.

Realization dawned on me. "It's because you healed me instead of your own wounds, isn't it?"

Leaning forward, Zyon placed a soft kiss on the tip of my nose. "Of course I healed you first. You are the most important thing to me, little one. Seeing you in pain was the worst agony I've ever experienced."

I'd dreamed of having someone care for me like this, and I had to swallow the lump of emotion in my throat. "Why didn't you bite me? You could have fed from me."

"Are you disappointed?" Zyon teased.

"Of course not." I stumbled over my denial. "I'd assumed it would be part of—you know—"

"No, I don't know what you're trying to say." Zyon raised an eyebrow.

"I thought biting would be part of having sex with a vampire!" I blurted out, my cheeks burning.

"I can see why you might think that, but you couldn't be further from the truth." Zyon brushed a strand of hair away from my face. "We never bite our partners."

"Never?" I squeaked as Zyon nuzzled my neck.

My body was still sore from our first bonding, but at his touch, something inside me perked up with interest. Maybe I could handle one more round...

"Never. It stems from our old customs. It's disrespectful to bite your partner and a sign of seeing them as less important."

"Why would they think less of them? Why should they even care?"

Zyon rubbed a clawed hand down his face. "Because vampires bite for food, and over time, we begin to see anything on our food chain as beneath us. Many vampires feel the same about a human feeder as humans feel about their chickens that lay eggs to eat or a cow that provides milk. They'll happily provide for needs, and they may even form an attachment, but the relationship between vampire and feeder isn't built on mutual respect."

Taking a deep breath, he continued, "Worse, it doesn't help that many humans have become vampire-obsessed groupies. Being bitten has become a kink for many humans.

This amuses vampires, but it also adds to our disdain for human feeders. A vampire who respects their partner would never dare drink from them. Also, feeding a vampire leaves the human weakened. A vampire would never want their mate to be in a vulnerable state."

"But what if both partners are vampires? Would they still be weakened?" I asked.

"Vampires cannot feed from each other. It would provide no nourishment since our cells require fresh blood." Zyon shuddered. "Also, vampires taste disgusting. We have absolutely no desire to take a nibble of each other."

I tried to stifle my laugh. "I'm not a vampire, so I shouldn't taste gross."

"Yes, I am well aware." Zyon's deep laugh sent a thrill through me.

"You're not a normal vampire. I don't need to protect myself as long as I'm with you. I know you'll protect me from an attack." It surprised me how confident I was that he'd spend his life trying to keep me safe.

"I would." He swallowed. "But I could also hurt you. I might take too much."

The longing to taste my blood was etched on his face. Zyon wanted to taste me.

"No, you won't. You've already shown your self-control," I tried to reassure him.

"I've shown very little self-control when it comes to you, little mate." His pained growl made my heart ache.

Whether he believed it or not, Zyon had shown incredible control. He could have easily injured me or even killed me the previous night. But he'd tenderly cradled my broken body, tended to my needs, and healed my wounds.

"So you have no desire to… taste me?" A week ago, if someone had told me I'd be trying to talk a vampire into feeding from me, I'd have laughed in their face. But Zyon needed to feed, and love made people do crazy things.

Zyon nipped my lip, careful not to break the skin. "I'm desperate to taste you." His voice was a harsh rasp.

"But you haven't…"

"No. And I won't." Zyon's voice was resolute, but his eyes burned with lust—or was that hunger?

My mouth decided that was the perfect time to speak the nine stupidest words I'd ever uttered. "But what if I wanted you to bite me?"

Zyon stopped breathing, and I fought the urge to facepalm. Why had I said that? The absolute last thing on earth I wanted to feel was Zyon's lips moving across my skin, his fangs puncturing my neck, or him licking and sucking while his hands caressed their way down my body…

"You're aroused. Again."

My cheeks flushed. "Gross. Do I smell bad?"

Zyon cleared his throat, and when he spoke, his voice was rough. "You smell heavenly." He rose quickly and backed away from the bed. "I need to go for a bit. To feed."

My heart tripped. "On someone else?"

Zyon's eyes were glued to the floor as he took another step away from me, his breathing ragged. "Yes."

Primal jealousy surged through me. I'd never been the

possessive type, so I struggled to process the unfamiliar but powerful emotion. "No."

Zyon stiffened. "What do you mean, no? I have to eat. I can't change that I'm a vampire, Tumbleweed."

"No." I shook my head, trying to clear the mess in my head. "I mean, I know that. I'm not asking you to starve yourself! I want you to eat from me. Only me."

His answer was immediate. "No."

I wasn't easily deterred, and the more I thought about his mouth on someone else, the more jealous I became. "Am I not enough? How many feeders does a vampire need?"

Zyon hesitated before answering. "One human is easily enough to keep a vampire alive. Unless the vampire is severely injured or burning through an incredible amount of energy."

"Then drink from me."

"Journee, I've already explained this. If I drink from you, you'll lose the respect of the other vampires. They'll think even less of you than they already do."

I snorted. "Do you really think I care what the other vampires think of me? Let me be clear. I don't care. Will you lose respect for me?"

"Of course not," Zyon snarled.

"Okay, so if it bothers you what the other vampires think of me, you could bite me somewhere less obvious…"

Zyon's silver eyes bled to red. Oh yes, he wanted what I was offering. I just needed to push a little bit more.

"You've already told me you're not a big fan of humans." I gave him a small smile, motioning at his massive gray form. "And we both know you can't go down the hall looking like that—not if you plan to keep this a secret."

Zyon stood as still as a statue, warring against his desire.

Taking a deep breath, I decided to be honest with him. "I don't want you to drink from anyone else. I know vampires see it as an emotionless exchange. At least on the vampire's part. But I can't handle knowing your lips are touching someone else. Only me. Zyon, you've offered me safety and protection. This is probably the only way I'll ever be able to provide for you."

That last statement roused him from his frozen state, and he blurred across the room to kneel in front of me. "You don't need to give me your blood. You've given me your heart and allowed me to bind our souls together. There is nothing more that I need."

"But I want to give you this." I slipped off the bed and scooted between his thighs.

"What are you doing?" There was wariness in both his tone and his eyes.

I pushed my long hair away from my neck and over my shoulder. "This is me showing you how much I trust you."

Zyon's pupils turned to razor-thin slits, and his breathing hitched.

Tilting my head to the side, I gave him what I hoped was a seductive look. "You healed my wounds. Let me help heal yours."

My monster's hand trembled as he reached out to cup

the back of my neck, showing how much my words and offering were affecting him. It was adorable, but I'd never tell him that.

Moving slowly, as though we had all the time in the world, he tenderly pressed his lips against the pulse on the side of my neck.

"You smell like heaven." Breathing deeply, he groaned. "What if I can't stop?"

"You will," I assured him. "You lie beside me all night without draining me in my sleep. I'm pretty sure you won't decide to kill me now." Trying to lighten the mood and ease his anxiety, I fluttered my eyelashes at him and teased, "Especially after you've put so much effort into keeping me alive."

"This is taboo." The powerful vampire's voice had dropped so low I could barely make out the words.

"And sometimes it's fun to be a little bit naughty," I whispered.

"I shouldn't." He said the words, almost pleading with me to stop him.

But I had no intention of stopping him.

Not wanting him to do something he'd be uncomfortable with, I asked, "Zyon, do you want to taste me?"

He was quiet for so long, I thought he wasn't going to answer. "I tasted your dried blood when I licked your wounds. It was unlike anything I'd ever tasted. I can't imagine how incredible the warm blood from your veins would taste."

It was the sweetest and grossest thing anyone had ever said to me. So why did it make my heart flutter?

Fear and excitement surged through me, and to my shock, I felt myself grow slick. Remembering how the layer of danger had added to my pleasure during our bonding the night before had my stomach twisting with lust.

Reaching up, I slid my fingers into his long, pale hair. I cradled his head tight against the slope between my neck and shoulder. "I've never been bitten by a vampire. No vampire has ever fed from me. I want you to be my first and only."

I'd found what Zyon couldn't resist, and his self-control snapped. Without preamble or warning, he sank his teeth deep into my skin.

I PROBABLY WOULD'VE BEEN MORE aware of the double row of sharp fangs sinking into my neck if not for the distraction of his fingers. Zyon had moved one of his long fingers between our bodies to stroke my clit at the same time he bit into my skin.

I cried out while my brain short-circuited from the shocking intensity of the sensations crashing through my body. There was a slight tug as Zyon sucked against my neck, drawing my blood into his mouth.

One thing I hadn't expected was the intensity of Zyon's

reaction. He moaned, and his massive body shuddered violently.

It was when he stiffened that I felt the first splash of something wet on my thighs. My first thought had been that I must have blood leaking from my neck.

Carefully angling my head in his hold, I managed to peek down at my lap, and my mouth fell open. Zyon's monster erection was spilling his seed as it pulsed between us.

Had he orgasmed just from tasting my blood? Vampires drank blood all the time, right? So drinking from me shouldn't have affected him this much. It wasn't like this was his first time sipping blood.

A horrible thought popped into my head. What if vampires had this reaction every time they drank from a human? If that were the case, Zyon would never drink from another human again.

My monster had fallen apart at the first taste of my blood, and that knowledge had my heart swelling with pride. He'd made feeding out to be more of an unemotional transaction, but in reality, this was insanely erotic.

Zyon's chest rumbled with a mixture of hungry growls and bliss-filled moans as he continued to devour me.

My fear of vampires had me slightly afraid Zyon might rip my skin and hungrily drain every last drop of blood from my veins. Instead, he was slow and gentle, as though he were savoring every mouthful.

I loved that I was sharing something so intimate with him—something neither of us had experienced before. Sure, he'd drunk from other humans. But never from his soulmate.

My desire uncurled, spreading through me, spurred on by the sexiness of our situation and the slight tinge of pain from his fangs buried in my skin. I moaned as his hand trailed down my bare back.

Zyon's hand moved to cup my breast. When his thumb brushed the hardened peak of my nipple, I arched against him.

We were completely lost to each other and the demand of the soulmate bond. The world could have been ending, but neither of us would have noticed.

Trailing my fingers through the sticky wetness on my thighs, I bumped against Zyon's monstrous anaconda. He'd already begun to grow hard again. How was that possible? Human males certainly didn't have this type of Olympic-level stamina.

This was definitely a plus to having a vampire mate. Yep. When it came to sex, humans sucked, and vampires ruled.

Although, technically, vampires were the ones who literally sucked.

Focusing back on Zyon's body, I tried to wrap my fingers around his girth but couldn't get my fingers to touch. Had he really fit inside me the night before? Maybe I had dreamed all of it.

For scientific purposes, I should probably try again... just to confirm we fit together as perfectly as I remembered.

Sliding my hand down his length elicited an appreciative rumble from Zyon. Encouraged by his reaction, I continued to stroke his erection. It was intoxicating how my touch caused his hot breath against my neck to grow more ragged.

The rough leather of his wings curved around my back, holding me close and reminding me I was in the lap of an honest-to-goodness monster. At any moment, his sharp fangs could rip out my throat. His long fingers wrapped in my hair could give a quick jerk and snap my neck.

He could kill me before I even had time to blink.

Yet, at that moment, I felt more powerful and in control than I ever had before.

Eager to drive my mate wild, I carefully lifted myself onto my knees without jostling my neck too much. Lining up Zyon's tip against my entrance, I eased down his hard length.

CHAPTER 3

zyon

Trying to resist Journee's offer to drink from her had been the worst kind of torture. My mouth had watered, and my fangs had ached with the overwhelming need to taste her blood.

It was incredibly taboo and wasn't something done among vampire partners, which should have made it easy to resist her offer. But knowing it was wrong made me want it even more.

Journee was offering me something no vampire would ever offer her mate, and it showed my Irenvyth's complete trust in me.

Eventually, my hunger, combined with the lust I felt for my little mate, was too much, and my resolve crumbled.

The moment my fangs sliced into her neck and her sweet taste danced across my tongue, I was lost in a torrent of passion.

I'd already been hard with need, and the intimacy of her blood in my mouth was my undoing. My body tightened, then spasmed from the explosive and unexpected orgasm that tore through me.

The lack of control was humiliating. I'd never come so fast, but I'd never experienced anything this erotic.

Was it because she was my Irenvyth—the other half of my soul?

I had no way of knowing. And since feeding from a soulmate was such a taboo topic, I couldn't risk asking anyone.

If drinking blood from your Irenvyth was the reason for the earth-rocking reaction, vampires were really missing out on the most intimate experience of their lives.

There was another possibility, though. It could be that Journee's blood was unique. Maybe it had created the orgasmic bliss that still shuddered through my body and already had my cock growing hard with need.

For a vampire, drinking blood was like sipping a glass of fine wine. Enjoyable, refreshing, flavorful, but not necessarily addictive. Some vampires were gluttons who lacked self-control, and eventually, they became the vampire version of an alcoholic.

However, most vampires were able to enjoy their liquid meals without losing control of themselves during the feeding.

But I'd never tasted anything like Journee's blood. It didn't possess a few flavorful notes like most human blood. No, her blood was an entire symphony in my mouth. Not only could I taste the music, but my mind and vision exploded into a full-color masterpiece.

That first tiny sip had sent strength surging through every muscle and fiber in my body. My mind had grown sharper, and my erection had hardened to the point of pain before erupting.

After drinking for a minute, I'd felt as though my body was primed to rock my soulmate's world or to murder an entire enemy army... or maybe both at the same time. I was already powerful, but the crackling energy pumping through my veins was exhilarating.

Tasting the sweet nectar in her veins, I was terrified I wouldn't be able to stop myself from taking every last drop. And if I, her fated mate, was struggling to keep from draining every last drop of blood from Journee, what if her blood had the same effect on other vampires?

No one could ever find out. I'd record myself dancing the Macarena while in my vampiric form on live television before I'd let someone find out about Journee's blood.

This was a secret that would cost my mate her life if it were to become known.

Moving my hand from between Journee's legs, I relished her petal-soft skin against mine as I explored her body. When my fingers found her breast, my gorgeous little mate arched against me.

Ever responsive to my touch, Journee's arousal flared, and my lungs were filled with the delectable vanilla and orange scent that was special to my mate.

Journee's fingers curled around my hyper-sensitive erection, and I groaned against her neck. When she slipped the head of my cock into her tight heat, I fought to keep my sucking gentle and not feed like a vampire starved.

Every vampire on earth knew they couldn't give in to bloodlust while experiencing sexual lust. But I was slipping further into the intoxicating fog of lust and hunger with each second.

I needed to pull away before I took too much. It was time to stop.

But how could I when every ounce of my being screamed in need for my mate?

For more of her blood and her body.

Wrapping my arm around her tiny waist, I pinned her against me. Thrusting hard, I sheathed myself deep, grinding our bodies together.

"Zyon," Journee whimpered, her hands sliding through my hair. "You feel so good."

I hummed in agreement, unable to speak with my fangs in her skin.

Journee was tight, her small body not meant to be bred by a monster. But fate had still chosen to bring us together. And if the adorable noises of pleasure coming from Journee's beautiful mouth were any indication, she didn't have any complaints about our size difference.

I needed it to stop.

I had to stop.

But I wanted so much more.

My mate's sweet blood slid down my throat and warmed my belly while our sweat-soaked bodies merged as one. Allowing my heavy eyelids to close, I committed every detail of this perfect moment to memory, so I could savor it for centuries to come.

Too soon, my body tightened with the need for release, spurred on by Journee's pleas for more. I plunged harder and deeper, driving us to our release.

Grabbing Journee's hips, I thrust one final time while hauling her hard against me. She screamed, her climax causing her tight channel to squeeze my length in a vice-like grip. Pulling my fangs from her neck, I bellowed her name as I followed her into bliss.

CHAPTER
4

journee

"S top worrying, you're going to do fine." Zyon's silky voice almost calmed my frayed nerves. Almost.

"Easy for you to say," I hissed up at him, trying not to get distracted by the way his silky pale hair fell over his silver eyes. "You're Zyon Timotei Milosovici, the freaking Crown Prince of the Vampire Kingdom. In case you've forgotten, I'm human. They are going to eat me alive."

Something darted across his face at the last sentence. Doubt? Worry? I couldn't place it, and I made a mental note to follow up on it later… when I wasn't on the verge of a mental meltdown.

"I'm the only one who will be eating you." Zyon's arm looped around my waist. "I promise we will eat quickly and return to our room."

The queen had sent Nathan to request Zyon's presence at breakfast. He wasn't supposed to have to appear until dinner, but she wanted him to welcome the castle's visitors this morning.

Zyon had planned to turn her down, but once he'd relaxed enough to shift back to his human-like form, I'd convinced him not to rock the boat with her. All our lives would be easier if she kept her word.

"It's fine." I was proud my voice sounded confident, even if my nerves already had my palms growing sweaty.

With each step we took, the sounds of feminine laughter and clattering dishes grew louder. My stomach began to pitch from side to side as though I were standing on a ship in the middle of a stormy sea. I'd be lucky to keep anything down.

"Prince Milosovici?" A guard dressed in crimson and gold appeared in front of us. "The queen requests your presence for a moment."

A second guard appeared at my elbow and offered me his arm. "Miss, I'm to escort you into the dining hall. The queen said there was no reason for you to starve while the prince attends to business."

"I will see the queen after breakfast." Zyon's voice was firm, and both guards hesitated.

"Prince, the queen was adamant that she meet with you before breakfast," the first guard insisted, looking as though he wished he could be anywhere else on earth other than delivering messages between two members of the royal family.

Zyon shook his head, but I patted his arm and smiled. "It will be fine. Remember, don't rock the boat. We only have to make it through two days."

Seeing their opening, the well-trained guards had us

moving in two different directions before we could change our minds.

The guard pushed open the large dining hall doors. One look inside was all it took for me to dig my heels in and bring both of us to a screeching halt.

"Miss? Is something wrong?" To his credit, the guard didn't appear annoyed, only concerned.

"I, uh…" I stammered, trying to find the words to explain why I couldn't go into that room.

I was having a textbook ugly duckling moment. There was no way I would fit in with the elegant—and fanged—swans filling the dining area. "Actually, I'm not hungry. I think I will just head back to my room. Could you tell the prince for me when he returns?"

The kindly, gray-haired guard studied me, and I squirmed. "Miss, the prince was taking you to eat and expects to return to find you here. I'm sure he will be at your side as soon as he finishes with the queen."

Still, I hesitated, the fizzy sensation rising from my stomach like a baking soda volcano preparing to explode.

"You needn't worry, miss. No one would dare attack a guest in the palace." Lines of sympathy creased his face, and I wondered how old a vampire had to be to show signs of aging.

The guard was trying hard to reassure me, but I was less worried about being eaten and far more worried about starring in a vampire spin-off of *Mean Girls*.

I'd known there were eligible women staying in the castle. But when he'd opened the doors to reveal close to fifty stunning vampires, reality had slammed into me like a grand piano in a Saturday morning cartoon.

Every single female in that room wanted Zyon.

My Zyon.

It was overwhelming, and my anxiety surged through the roof. I rested my hand on my churning stomach and swallowed back a hiccup.

Worse, how was I going to compete with these women? How could Zyon resist the sheer perfection that was being offered to him on a golden platter?

Glancing down at my clothing, I took a step back. I was going to stick out like a sore thumb, and not just because I was human.

"I think it's best that I go back to my room. It appears I'm not really dressed for a royal breakfast." I tried to pull my hand free of the guard's arm, but his hand patted mine reassuringly.

"The prince couldn't take his eyes off you, miss. I'd say what you're wearing is perfect."

The guard was wearing polished silver armor and crushed red velvet. I was wearing my favorite pair of ripped jeans and an oversized AC/DC sweatshirt. We were not the same.

"Easy for you to say," I mumbled, forgetting he had vampiric hearing.

The guard chuckled and motioned to my shirt. "That's one of my favorite bands since Mozart. He was a rockstar before it was cool. The parties he threw are still unrivaled. Such a great guy."

My jaw dropped at the casual way he named dropped celebrities from centuries ago.

The guard continued, "Also, I guarantee you are far more comfortable than any of the ladies in that room."

I rubbed the fabric of my well-worn tee between my fingers. Nathan had been kind enough to collect my clothes after cleaning up the mess at my apartment. This morning when I'd dressed, I'd reached for my comfort clothes.

Maybe I was weird, but I found my ridiculously soft and comfy clothes calming, in much the same way comfort food sometimes calmed my anxiety or stress. But I wasn't chilling in my living room. This was the freakin' vampire castle.

Zyon had been kissing me while I'd dressed, and somehow, in my distraction, I'd forgotten to anticipate how dressed up everyone else would be.

Men didn't always think about things like dress codes, and what if I ended up embarrassing him? I hiccupped.

The guard gently tugged me toward the doorway again. "I think Prince Zyon wouldn't be happy to find you in the hall second-guessing yourself."

"Thanks a lot, Dr. Phil." My snort turned into another hiccup. "Do you moonlight as a psychologist?"

"My name is Turik, not Phil. I just happen to have lived long enough that I am pretty darn good at reading people." The guard chuckled. "And miss? Never play poker. Your face is far too expressive."

I started to stick out my tongue at his teasing, then

thought better of it and ducked my head so he wouldn't see me blush.

"Fine. Let's get this over with," I mumbled between hiccups.

The hiccups were getting exhausting. Maybe I should see a doctor about them since they were going to be a pain in the butt as long as I was spending time in a palace filled with vampires.

Actually, Zyon and I hadn't talked about where we would be living permanently.

I knew I could never go back to my apartment after the attack. While I didn't follow celebrity vampire gossip, I knew enough to know the prince didn't reside at the palace full-time. So where did he live?

My stomach quivered, and a sliver of doubt swirled inside my chest. We'd bound ourselves together in a way that was far more permanent than marriage, yet I didn't even know where he lived.

I didn't know Zyon's favorite color, his hobbies, his least favorite food, his favorite joke, his most cherished child-hood memories... I knew he liked garlic. And me.

But I would bet money that every woman in the dining hall knew more about Zyon than I did. They'd studied him with more fervor than a CIA agent prepping for a world-saving mission.

How could I hope to compete?

I remembered the way he'd rescued me, the way he'd held me through nightmares, the way he'd made love to me. My chest warmed with love.

The competition was already over.

Zyon was mine.

I just needed to stay focused on that, and I would survive these next two days.

Lifting my chin, I squeezed Turik's arm. "Let's do this."

"Okay, miss." He gave me a teasing salute.

"Not *miss*, just Journee," I corrected, returning his smile.

Turik barked a laugh. "The prince would have my head for that, Miss Journee."

We entered the dining hall, and I tried to keep my expression calm as a cucumber. My internal warning system was working overtime, thanks to the two dozen vampires milling about the room.

Looking around at the unfamiliar faces, my unease grew, and my hiccups picked up their chaotic tempo.

"Here we go!" Turik guided me toward an empty table near the buffet. "I always love sitting as close as possible to the food. It makes getting a second—and third—plate easier."

Giving him a wobbly smile, I sank down onto a gold-cushioned chair. Realizing I was going to be alone in a room of strangers, I nearly panicked. "Are you going to sit?"

"I'm on duty, miss. But I will be standing near the door. If you need anything, just shout, and I'll be at your side faster than you can blink." Turik gave me a slight bow, and before I could protest, he blurred across the room to take up his post.

"You're a grownup. You can handle this." I mumbled encouragement to myself, hoping to trick my brain into

41

believing me. "Pretend it's a business meeting. You've sat through a few of those and survived."

Except this was nothing like those boring business meetings. My eyes slid around the room, taking in the old-world opulence and decor.

This was the type of room you'd expect to see on a tour of an old palace. A room you peeked at while standing behind the silk rope keeping visitors from touching the priceless furniture and antique decor.

Individual tables were scattered around the room, each adorned with a bouquet of no less than three dozen roses in the middle. Delicate china trimmed in gold, and hand-painted with an elegant floral design, was set on each table.

Along the wall nearest me was the largest buffet I'd ever laid eyes on. It ran the full length of the wall, and while measurements weren't my strong point, it had to be at least forty feet in length.

At any other time in my life, I would've rushed toward the lavish display of food... I was a girl in love with food of all types. But with my stomach flopping around like a fish on dry land, I doubted I'd be able to keep anything down.

Pulling my longing gaze away from the mouthwatering buffet, I studied the women flitting around the room like a colorful gaggle of geese.

Their porcelain skin was free of laugh lines, crow's feet, or blemishes. Every single lady's eyes were bright and glittered with excitement. Shiny hair of nearly every shade was scattered around the room, and there wasn't a split end in sight.

Yep. There was no denying that vampires possessed an other-worldly beauty.

Don't get me wrong. I'd been told I was good-looking, but I wasn't delusional either. My hair was sleek… right up until I stepped outside into the humidity. And let's not talk about the split ends that no amount of YouTube hair care tutorials had managed to repair.

My skin was nice, other than during shark week, when I tended to break out and have flashbacks to my teenage years. And to my unending annoyance, no amount of sleep had been able to get rid of the circles under my eyes.

I was a catch, but I was no vampiric princess, and this room was playing havoc on my self-esteem.

My hands grew sweaty, and I discreetly wiped them with my cloth napkin beneath the cover of the cloth table skirt.

I must have gotten something on my skin because the fabric stuck to my hand as though there was syrup on my palm.

"How weird…" I yanked hard, trying to pull the napkin free, but to no avail.

"Hi. I don't think we've met before."

My head jerked up at the silky voice, and I found a smiling vampire had settled into the seat across from me. While I knew she was a vampire, she looked more like a fairy with her heart-shaped face, perfect cupid's bow lips, aquamarine eyes, and golden hair that fell to her waist.

Ever eloquent, I stammered, "Um, no?"

I tucked my hands between my thighs to hide my predicament.

Tilting her head, she studied me for a moment before her eyebrows lifted. "You're human?"

It was a weird way to open a conversation, but not wanting to create a stir, I nodded. "Yes. I've been a part of the immortality-challenged since my birth."

My response must have caught the vampire off guard, because she burst into laughter.

"What's your name, human?" The corner of her mouth quirked up at the last word, letting me know she was teasing, rather than insulting, me.

I returned her smile. "I'm Journee, and you?"

"I'm Kelsey. It's definitely my pleasure to meet you, Journee." She leaned forward, resting her chin on her hands and grinning. "At the risk of sounding terribly rude, what are you doing here?"

I couldn't hide my snort. "I don't think you care about whether you sound rude or not."

"Fine, you've caught me." Kelsey lifted her hands in mock surrender. "But it's fairly well known the prince is less than fond of humans. And since this whole shindig was arranged for the queen to force marriage on him, I can't figure out where you fit."

"Yes. Well." Honestly, I didn't know what else to say. 'I kind of forced my company on him?' or, 'By the way, I'm his soulmate?'

Nope. Even though they were the truth, neither of those explanations would work.

I was saved from the awkward pause when Nathan's chipper voice came from across the room.

"Hey there, human!" Nathan flashed his fangs in a lazy smile as he swaggered toward us.

"You know Nathan?" Kelsey's blue eyes darted between us.

I could practically hear the gears turning in her head as she tried to figure out how I fit into this puzzle.

Sighing, I narrowed my eyes at Nathan. "What is it with you guys calling me human? Just so you know, it's pretty unoriginal."

"Apologies, my lady." In a polite gesture that was totally not him, Nathan lifted my hand and kissed the back of my hand. "It may be unoriginal, but your reaction is hilarious."

Turning, he lifted Kelsey's hand to his lips. "Good morning, Countess Du Pont."

Their gazes locked, and he held her hand just a little too long to be considered casual.

Were they attracted to each other?

Well, well, well. This was an interesting development.

One thing didn't make sense, though. If Kelsey was at the castle to capture the prince's heart, why was a blush spreading across her cheeks as Nathan's lips pressed against her hand?

"I've told you to call me Kelsey." The vampiress' voice had taken on a breathless note.

"That was more than thirty years ago," Nathan responded. "I didn't want to presume the offer still stood."

"Of course it does. Nothing has changed." The catch in

Kelsey's voice made me suspect she wasn't just talking about her giving him permission to call her by her first name.

Had they been friends? Lovers?

I was going to have a list of questions to ask Zyon next time we were alone.

At the thought of my mate, I glanced around, hoping to catch sight of the sexy prince. From across the room, Turik gave a subtle shake of his head, letting me know the prince hadn't arrived.

Nathan dropped into an empty chair at our table.

"So, how do you two know each other?" Kelsey's fingers fidgeted with the gold-plated silverware. Would that make it goldware instead of silverware?

Regardless, the fidgeting betrayed her nerves. Was that a hint of jealousy I spied with my little eyes?

Unsure of how to respond, I shot a quick look at Nathan.

"Now that is a funny story." Nathan smirked. "But I think we'd better feed the human rather than delve into that particular tale before we've had caffeine."

Standing, Nathan held out a hand to each of us. "Shall we?"

CHAPTER 5

journee

After filling our plates to overflow with what seemed to be every type of fruit and pastry in existence, we returned to our chairs.

Having Nathan sitting at the table helped to calm some of my nerves, and I found myself ravenously hungry. In fact, I was hungrier than I'd ever been in my life. Maybe sex with a vampire burned a lot of calories.

If that was the case, I was going to be in great shape, and I was going to go ahead and cancel my gym membership… or I would have, if I'd had a gym membership.

The clearing of a throat echoed through the room, and in an instant, everyone fell silent. A guard stepped through the open doorway.

"Crown Prince Zyon Timotei Milosovici," the guard announced before stepping to the side and allowing Zyon to step into the dining room.

A ripple of awed gasps traveled around the room, and I knew why.

Because I felt the same thrill of excitement.

Zyon was a magnificent specimen of manhood. I was beginning to understand why there were countless fan clubs dedicated to him and why there was a room of gorgeous, wealthy vampire females willing to throw themselves at him.

To be fair, I couldn't judge them since I'd thrown myself at him. Literally.

Although I'd been motivated by pure fear. Not lust. Fine, I couldn't deny there had been a bit of lust.

After all, I could've thrown myself at Nathan or one of the other guys. But I'd run straight into Zyon's arms. Was that due to the pull of the mate bond?

Faces that had been animated and calculating before Zyon's entrance turned seductive. Around the room, women played with their hair, leaning forward to give him a better view of their cleavage.

Jealousy bloomed in my chest, a burning ache that begged for violence. It was intimidating having a room full of women undressing your man with their eyes and trying their best to draw his attention.

Zyon's silver gaze scanned the room, finding mine within seconds. Without giving anyone else in the room a second look, he headed straight for me.

My jealousy faded. Mostly.

"Looks like Zyon only has eyes for one woman in this room," Kelsey whispered behind me.

Zyon reached my table. Leaning down, he caught my lips in a hungry kiss.

I'd expected him to act like we were merely acquaintances. Instead, he'd come straight to me and kissed me as though we were lovers.

Which we totally were, but I thought we were keeping that a secret.

Pulling back, I stared up at him in confusion. "This wasn't part of the plan, Zyon." I blew out a shaky breath. "You're supposed to play it cool. Remember?"

"I couldn't help myself." Zyon's heated look had my insides quivering.

How long until breakfast was over? I needed to drag him back to his room and devour him.

"Let me grab some food, and I'll be right back." Zyon straightened, grabbed an empty plate from our table and made his way to the buffet.

He barely placed the first pastry on his plate before nearly every woman in the room descended on him. They surrounded him like a school of starving piranhas, ready to eat the meat from his bones.

Hiccupping, I fought back a fresh surge of jealousy. I was the only one allowed to eat his meat and bones. My stomach twisted, and I wished I'd resisted the urge to eat that second icing-covered caramel-drizzled bear claw.

"Poor Zyon."

Lost in my thoughts, I'd jumped at Nathan's comment.

"The poor guy's face looks like he's wading through waist-deep mud while surrounded by feces-covered pigs," Kelsey added with a giggle.

I squinted, taking a second look at the scene in front of me. They were right. Zyon looked absolutely disgusted.

When a particularly pushy woman reached out to lay her hand on his chest, Zyon brushed it away with a shudder.

Once again, that uncomfortable flicker of jealousy burning in my chest melted away.

I was the girl he'd kissed. Zyon didn't want them.

He only wanted me.

Zyon pulled out the chair next to mine and sat down. "You should eat more, Tumbleweed. Do you need me to feed you?"

The purr in his words sent a sharp spasm of need through me. Unable to speak, I shook my head. Reaching out a shaky hand, I picked up a cookie with a dab of orange marmalade in the middle of it.

Zyon's gaze never left mine as I ate the cookie. When I'd finished, his thumb touched the corner of my mouth, wiping away the tiniest bit of jelly before softly pressing it to my lips for me to lick clean.

Forgetting there were other people in the room and completely lost in the moment, I took things a step further and sucked his thumb into my mouth. My tongue circled the rough skin of his finger, and I watched in glee as his irises shifted from an icy gray to a molten silver.

Kelsey's shocked gasp brought me back to reality.

"Wait! How'd I miss it? This is the woman from the viral photo, isn't it?" Kelsey whispered. "No wonder she smells like him."

"Yep." Nathan popped the *p*. "She's the one and only."

"I can see that." From the corner of my eye, I caught the slight sag in Kelsey's shoulders.

Her expression didn't seem disappointed. She almost appeared to be relieved. Why was Kelsey here if she didn't want a chance at becoming Zyon's bride?

I didn't get a chance to ask.

"Zyon, darling!" A woman with the voice of a Hollywood starlet appeared at Zyon's side.

It wasn't the fact that she'd called him *darling* that had me seeing red. No, it was the way she wrapped her arms around Zyon's neck and leaned in for a kiss that had fury boiling inside me.

The internal red flags which had been warning me of the nearby vampiric danger switched to green, giving me the go-ahead to take her out.

Take her out? I gave myself a mental shake. When had I become so violent?

I needn't have worried.

"Remove your arms from my body, or I will remove them from yours." Zyon's harsh tone was one I hadn't heard him use, and although he wasn't talking to me, I instinctually shrank away from him.

The brown-haired vampire yanked her hands away from him so fast she stumbled backward a step. She quickly recovered, and with a grace I envied, tucked her brown shoulder-length hair behind her ear.

"You've always had a flair for the dramatic." Her lips pursed in an exaggerated pout. "I know it's been a century since we last saw each other, but there's no need to act like we're strangers."

"It has been two centuries, and still not long enough." Zyon refused to even look in her direction.

Picking up a plump grape from my plate, Zyon held it to my lips. I opened my mouth, allowing him to feed me. It was intimate, and I gloated more than a little on the inside, knowing the vampire female was watching.

The urge to kill her eased.

Slightly.

"Ella, the prince is busy right now. Maybe this isn't the right time to chat about old times." Nathan stood, and, ignoring her protests, led her away.

"You're going to owe Nathan for that." Kelsey raised a teacup to her lips to hide a smirk.

Zyon pinched the bridge of his nose, sighing heavily. "Without a doubt. He will remind me of this for at least a century."

Zyon reached out, catching my hand in his. "I can't believe my grandmother invited her."

"You can't blame the queen." Kelsey wrinkled her nose. "As much as it pains me to say it, Ella is considered the most eligible and sought-after vampiress. If the queen hadn't invited Ella, her family would have been out for blood and retaliation for the perceived insult."

"Why is she the most eligible? You're a countess, right?" I really should have spent more time studying vampire society gossip, but how was I supposed to know I'd end up engaged and bound to the prince?

Kelsey shrugged. "I have a title and a nice family line, but Ella Wessex's family line is far older, possesses staggering wealth, and has established a legacy as powerful leaders within vampiric politics. The Wessex family raised her to believe she'd become the next vampire queen. Now she thinks she is owed the throne, and she wants the crown, and Zyon, with a rabid hunger."

Pain sizzled through me like lightning, and my hands grew sweaty again. Searching the room, I found Ella standing in a corner. Nathan was blocking her from returning to the table, but our eyes connected.

THREAT.

The single word echoed inside my mind, causing my breathing to quicken and my hiccups to return with a vengeance.

But something was different. This time, instead of my mind screaming for me to run away from the vampires, I wanted to run straight toward her and...

And what? I bit back a laugh at the idiocy of my thoughts. What on earth did I think I was going to do to her? Ella would happily swat me down as though I were an annoying gnat before I managed to lay a finger on her.

"Journee, look at me." I wanted to obey Zyon's command, but I couldn't drag my attention from the vampire female who wanted my soulmate.

When I didn't look at him, Zyon caught my chin between his fingers and forced me to look at him. "Breathe, my love. Ella means nothing to me. None of these women do."

"Did you have sex with her?" I blurted out my deepest fear before I could stop myself.

Zyon's eyes widened in horror, but it was Kelsey's reaction that surprised me. The sophisticated blonde choked on her tea, spewing it out.

"Crap! Warn a girl before you say something like that, Jo," Kelsey wheezed between coughs while frantically wiping up the mess she'd made.

We'd moved onto nicknames already?

"It was a serious question, *Kels*." I checked for Kelsey's response, but she just smiled. "Besides, I'm not sure what's so funny," I grumbled, waiting for Zyon to find his voice.

"What's going on?" Nathan dropped back into his chair and studied our faces. "And why does Zyon look like someone kicked him in the balls?"

"Journee asked him if he'd done the rumpy-pumpy with Ella," Kelsey whispered.

"Gross! No wonder he looks like he is about to vomit!" Nathan barked out a laugh. "Zyon has spent his entire life playing the world's longest game of hide-and-seek with Ella and the entire Wessex family."

"But why? If she's such a perfect match?" I didn't add that she was the most stunning woman I'd ever laid eyes on, but I definitely thought it.

Kelsey leaned toward me and dropped her voice. "There's nothing wrong with having your vagina listed as a check-in place on social media, but if Ella had as many pricks sticking out of her as she's had stuck in her, she'd look like a porcupine."

Nathan coughed into his hand but failed to hide his laughter. "Ella is spoiled. When the queen turned down the

Wessex's betrothal proposal when Zyon and Ella were teenagers, Ella began a mission to make him want her."

Kelsey picked up the story. "Ella wants whatever she can't have. Thinking she could make Zyon jealous, she began a new game. When she found a vampire male she wanted, she relentlessly pursued him until she seduced him. The few times she has been in a relationship, she dumped her partner the minute someone richer came along. But she continues to believe Zyon will come to his senses and propose to her when he sees how sought-after she is."

Zyon shifted in his seat, clearing his voice. "I have many reasons for not wanting to accept an offer of marriage from the Wessex family." Zyon paused.

He couldn't marry someone and keep his monster a secret. But was that the only reason?

"I am not attracted to her, and we have nothing in common. I can't imagine being in an eternal marriage with her." Zyon shuddered. "When we were young, my grandmother thought the betrothal was a smart arrangement, but her eyes were opened to Ella's character quickly, and she stopped suggesting I consider the match."

A waiter appeared at the table, holding a tray of bubbly mimosas. Zyon tried to pull his hand from mine to pluck a glass flute from the tray, only to frown when his hand stayed firmly in mine.

I tried to uncurl my fingers to let go of his hand, but we were stuck. What on earth had I touched? Panic shot through me. Was someone pranking me with glue? How was I going to explain this?

The napkin had eventually loosened and fallen free, so maybe the glue was only sticky when wet from my constant nervous sweating?

If that was the case, as long as I didn't get stressed out again, our hands should do the same.

Hopefully.

For now, I needed to play it cool. Tightening my fingers around his, I pretended I just didn't want to let him go.

Zyon shot me a suspicious glance but relaxed his left hand in mine. Lifting his right hand, he grabbed a glass from the tray. He took a long drink before setting the glass on the table. All the while, his thumb stroked the back of my hand in a soothing gesture.

Wanting to change the topic, I asked, "What did the queen want when you went to see her?"

"To remind me of our agreement in order to avoid a political scandal. I'm to be kind to all the visiting vampiresses and wait until after tomorrow to announce"—he paused, remembering Kelsey was sitting at our table and finished lamely—"things."

"Things like you two are in love, and no one here has a chance at winning the prince's heart?" Kelsey winked at me.

"You aren't upset?" Curious about her reaction, I whispered, although, with the racket from the clattering buffet dishes and noise from multiple conversations going on, I doubted anyone could hear us.

Kelsey waved away my question. "I don't want your man."

"Then why are you here?" I took the opportunity to ask what I'd been wondering since she'd sat down at my table.

"Because it was easier to come than to listen to my family's incessant nagging and complaints if I refused. Plus, I knew this was bound to be better than reality TV. The world's most reclusive and eligible bachelor, forced to spend a week with a castle full of women all intent on winning his hand." Kelsey leaned back in her chair and grinned. "Now that I know Zyon has already chosen his bride, I know this will be even more entertaining."

I liked Kelsey, and I could certainly use a female friend in the castle, so it was a relief to know she wasn't my competition.

Zyon rolled the stem of his empty glass between his fingers. "This is a ridiculous farce, and I told the queen so."

Nathan leaned forward to pat Zyon's shoulder. "You only have to keep it together for another two days. How hard can that be?"

"It's torture," Zyon growled. "I'm already getting a headache from the incessant noise."

Nathan chuckled. "The rest of the guys will be here in a few hours, and we will protect you from the mind-numbing small talk."

It was meant as a joke, but Zyon's expression was serious. "Yes, I'd appreciate that." Turning to me, Zyon added, "Let's head back to my room before I end up with a migraine."

Still gripping my hand, Zyon stood, pulling me to my feet. He gave a quick bow to Kelsey and Nathan before leading me from the dining room.

Zyon might not have noticed the glares being sent my way, but I could feel the furious daggers that were being stared into my back.

Vampires had incredible hearing, which made me wonder how much of our conversation had been overheard. I doubted very much, thanks to the relentless noise echoing around the room.

So did they hate me because I was human, or was it because the prince was still holding my hand?

CHAPTER 6

journee

"You're finished, miss. I'll have my assistant call Zyon to let him know you are ready for him to return." Jamis, the castle tailor, snapped his measuring tape.

"Don't worry about it. I know how to get back to his room from here." With a groan, I stretched my aching back. "How do you do this every day? This was exhausting, and all I did was stand around and watch you work!"

"Of course you're exhausted. Being that beautiful must be exhausting." Jamis grinned at my embarrassment and continued his teasing. "I'm happily married. Otherwise, I might have tried to steal you from the prince."

"Shh! You aren't supposed to know about us," I whispered to my newest friend.

Jamis rolled his eyes. "If I wasn't supposed to know, why'd the queen commission me to make a wedding dress for you? Hmm?"

"WHAT?" I nearly toppled off the pedestal I'd been standing on.

Jamis caught my hand, steadying me as I stepped down. "You didn't know? Oops. I really shouldn't be trusted with secrets."

"No, I didn't know." I bent to gather my jeans and T-shirt from the floor.

When I'd first been handed off to Jamis, I'd been embarrassed to have him pinning and measuring my nearly naked body, but he'd eased my discomfort with his professional yet easy-going personality.

Plus, Jamis had talked so much about his partner, it was clear he was in love and had zero interest in my body.

When he'd asked me to remove my clothes to get my exact measurements, I'd been relieved Zyon had the foresight to cover his bite mark on my neck. It had nearly healed, but the skin was still raised and slightly pink... and obviously a vampire bite.

"Is it okay?" For the first time in the past six hours, Jamis was serious. "I've always wanted to design a royal wedding dress, but I understand if that was overstepping."

"Are you kidding?" Throwing my arms around Jamis's neck, I squealed. "I'm so happy you're making my gown! I can't think of anyone I'd trust more. And it is a relief, since I'm clueless when it comes to royal fashion."

"Yay!" Jamis spun me around. "I swear it will be the most incredible wedding gown the castle has ever seen! And can I just tell you how relieved I am that I'm designing the gown for you and not for that horrible Wessex brat?"

Jamis set me on my feet, laughing when I wobbled drunkenly.

"Maybe we should discuss a budget? I will probably be paying this dress off for the next twenty years—"

"You hush, missy! The queen has given me permission to design your gown without concern regarding costs. And the prince has put me in charge of your wardrobe. I'm allowed to create anything I want or think you might need. You will be the Jackie Kennedy of the vampire kingdom. Prince Zyon gave me the go-ahead to contact my favorite makeup artist and hair stylist to join your personal team." Jamis rubbed his hands together in delight. "Your gorgeous little figure will be on the cover of every magazine and featured in every celebrity blog in the world. Everyone will want to copy your style."

This time, the wobble in my legs wasn't from dizziness. "Jamis. I'm a small-town farm girl. I don't know if I can do this."

Terrifying visions of embarrassing the royal family on such a public scale flashed through my mind.

"Doll, that is what will make you even more likable! Marilyn Monroe was a small-town girl too, and she is an icon."

I'd gone from being a secondhand clothing store sales-girl, to considering working on a coconut farm, to becoming part of the vampire royal family. It was a lot to take in.

Stepping into my jeans, I wiggled them over my hips.

"I've already finished the sketches of your wedding dress. Would you like to see? That way, I could make changes if you want." Jamis moved to a desk covered in needles, scraps of fabric, and various sparkling beads and crystals.

I pulled my shirt over my head. "Nope. I want to be surprised. I know it will be incredible."

Jamis turned and leaned back against the desk, his green eyes sparkling. "It will be the most incredible dress I've ever made. I've canceled all my other work to focus on your wardrobe and wedding gown. The prince might even pass out when he sees you walking toward him."

It was amazing that although the tailor was a vampire, I hadn't hiccupped or sweated in his studio. My warning system was still on alert, but it wasn't pushing me to run. Jamis was just a genuinely kind guy.

Pulling my hair back in a ponytail, I rushed to Jamis' side and gave him a kiss on the cheek. "I'll never be able to thank you enough."

"Don't worry about that. The queen and the prince will compensate me well. And I can already tell we are going to be besties—which is a relief. I'm sick of dealing with entitled wannabe royalty, and I'd rather focus on you." Jamis made the shooing motion. "But you better get out of here. I need to finish altering the gown you'll wear to dinner tonight."

"I'm going, I'm going!" I giggled and made my way out into the castle hallway.

I HEADED down the hall toward Zyon's room but stopped when I turned a corner and nearly collided with a group of vampire women. They fell silent when they spotted me.

The tallest female tilted her nose into the air as though I were a servant. "What are you doing here? Humans are supposed to be in the feeding room."

"I'm not a feeder." I moved to step by the three women, but a second vampire blocked my way.

Flustercuck. I was too tired to deal with this, and already the fizzy bubbles were swirling in my stomach. All I wanted was a nap before dinner. Was that too much to ask?

"Wait. This is the human who left with Prince Zyon this morning." The vampiress blocking my way stepped closer. "Where'd you two run off to?"

The third female laughed, a shrill sound that scraped against my eardrums. "Where do you think, Molly? A man like the prince has needs, and being in the room with all those female pheromones likely got his instincts stirred up. He would need a plaything to take out those needs on."

The first female looked me up and down, lip curling. "Is that true? Are you the prince's whore? I assure you, he won't need your services once he finally settles down with me."

The second female giggled. "I think you mean when he picks me!"

My warning system was flickering between red alert and green, and I was getting a migraine from the noise in my mind.

63

KILL.
RUN.
FIGHT.
FLEE.

Taking another step forward, I tried to move around the vampires. The taller female blurred straight into me, tossing me into the stone wall with a hard crack.

I was proud when I still managed to land on my feet, despite my surprise and the sudden pain.

The vampiress leaned in until our noses nearly touched.

"Maybe you should get glasses if you need to get this close to see me," I snarled.

"You insolent piece of trash." She spat in my face.

The odd thing was, I knew she was going to spit a split second before she did it. I knew deep in my gut I could have moved her out of the way before it hit my cheek. But I chose not to move, a tiny voice warning me not to reveal my ability.

Not yet.

Her wet spit hit my cheek, then slid to the floor. I swallowed my rage and my hiccup and raised my brow. "Are you finished with your tantrum?"

Heck! Where had this backbone come from? I couldn't decide if I was proud of myself, or if I wanted to rip it out and beat myself with it. Why on earth was I goading a vampire?

"You're mouthy for a human! Do you think you deserve special treatment just because you're the prince's toy?"

I tapped my chin as though deep in thought. "If you're

waiting for me to care what you think of me, I hope you brought something to eat... because you'll be waiting a long time."

"Maybe I'll just eat you!" Her eyes bled to black, and her fangs descended as her form shifted.

Grabbing my shirt, she hauled me forward, and I winced at the sound of tearing fabric.

I loved this shirt.

The simmering anger pushed past my restraints, and pain rippled through my chest cavity. Either I had a case of heartburn from hell, or something was wrong with me.

Maybe I was having a heart attack from fear. No, that couldn't be it, because I wasn't afraid at all. I was seething and wanted to fight.

I'm not sure what would have happened had Turik not rounded the corner, started shouting and stepped between me and the angry vampires.

"Miss Journee is an invited guest. No different from any of you. Show some decency!" Turik hissed at the female vampires.

"How was I supposed to know? I thought only vampires of the kingdom had been invited!" the vampiress with her claws in my shirt snarled back.

"See? This is why you and Monday are similar—nobody likes either of you," Kelsey growled, striding toward us from the opposite end of the hallway.

Dang. Kelsey wasn't dealing with their bull.

In my mind, I cheered her on.

The vampiress released my shirt, stepping away from

the angry guard who'd rested his hand on the hilt of his sword.

Her stormy expression darkened further, but turning on her heel, she flounced away with the other two women following behind her.

Turik, Kelsey and I watched them go.

Kelsey was the one to break the silence. "I don't know what her problem is, but I bet it's something super hard to pronounce."

CHAPTER 7

journee

The dinner that evening was uneventful. Word must have spread through most of the vampires that I was a guest, and other than some nasty looks, they left me alone.

Since Zyon refused to leave my side, they wouldn't have had much of an opportunity to attack me anyway. After three hours of dealing with mindless small talk, fluttering eyelashes, and countless innuendos, Zyon called it quits and excused himself.

Completely exhausted from the evening, I was relieved when we were able to sneak away to Zyon's room.

"This was the longest night of my life," I groaned, pushing open the bedroom door and stumbling inside.

I needed to talk to Jamis about giving me shorter heels if I was going to be attending official events in the future.

"Agreed," Zyon called from the closet where he was hanging up his suit jacket.

Kicking off my heels, I turned toward the bed, and my blood froze in my veins.

"Zyon." I tried to keep my voice from trembling, but fear made it impossible. "Someone has been in here."

"How do you know—" Zyon stepped from the closet.

His chest expanded as he took in a deep breath. In an instant, his arms wrapped around me like bands of steel, and his chest vibrated with a vicious growl.

Safe in Zyon's embrace, I searched the rest of the bedroom. It didn't feel like anyone was still in the room, but something evil lingered in the air.

Maybe I was overreacting. Besides, there was no way I should be able to tell if someone had been in the room.

My eyes returned to the tiny box on the bed. Taking a deep breath, I ducked from under Zyon's arms and walked straight to the side of the bed.

There, on the top flap, was my name written in elegant calligraphy.

Picking it up, I turned it in my trembling hand. There was nothing evil about the pink box, but darkness seemed to emanate from it.

Zyon appeared at my side and snatched the box from my hand.

"Let me open it. If it's a bomb, I'll survive. You won't." His voice was tight, and his features were set in grim lines.

My hand unconsciously wrapped around my neck, and I voiced my biggest fear. "Do you think it was Abner?"

"No. He's dead." Zyon sounded sure, but the angry clench of his jaw had me questioning him.

Zyon savagely tore apart the cardboard. The paper fell away, revealing a ring. With a snarl, he yanked the ring from the velvet and held it up. As he turned it in his fingers, the diamond surrounded by emeralds sparkled in the firelight.

A note fluttered from the bed, and I bent to pluck it from the floor.

My darling Journee,
We waited so long for our first time alone together, and it crushes
my soul that we were interrupted. The vampiric abomination has
stolen much from us, but I won't allow it to continue. Be patient,
my sweet. Our love is strong enough to survive this temporary
setback. Let this ring be a reminder that you belong to me and
that I'll have you by my side soon.
Abner

"No!" I shrieked until my throat was raw.

Terror and anguish threatened to consume me as my hot tears trailed down my cheeks, soaking the scrap of paper.

"He's supposed to be dead! Why isn't he dead?" Violent tremors rocked my body, and my teeth clattered together.

The room shook, and the walls groaned from the power of Zyon's roar. Through my veil of tears, I watched his face transform into a mask of uncontrolled fury.

Cursing in an ancient language I didn't understand, Zyon flung the ring into the fireplace.

In the next moment, Zyon lifted me so my legs were around his waist and pinned me up against a wall. "My Irenvyth, that man will never touch you again."

I sobbed, clinging to my soulmate. "He was in here, Zyon. In our room."

Zyon's chest heaved, his breathing harsh. "And I will figure out how that happened so it doesn't happen again. Journee, I will protect you."

All the terror and pain I'd felt at Abner's hand, and his knife, came rushing back. I couldn't go through that again.

My stalker was insane, and now we knew he was still alive.

Abner wasn't going to leave me alone. Not until one of us was dead.

My breathing came in fast pants, and the world tilted as a wave of dizziness swirled in my skull. I was going to pass out. Rather than fight it, I welcomed the bliss of nothingness with open arms.

"I'M NOT GOING to wake her up. She went into shock, and her body needs the sleep."

Zyon's voice came from somewhere in the distance.

A different voice murmured something, but I couldn't make out the words.

With effort, I managed to crack open my eyes. "Zyon?"

The bed shifted, and Zyon's finger traced my jawline. "I didn't mean to wake you, Tumbleweed."

"I heard you talking to someone?" My head throbbed

with a building migraine. There was something I was forgetting. Something important, but it stayed just out of reach.

"Nathan is here, but he's leaving. You can go back to sleep." Zyon's lips brushed against mine.

"The queen—" Nathan's words were clearer this time.

Groaning, I tried to sit up, but Zyon pressed me gently back down on the bed.

"You should rest." Zyon sounded concerned, but I couldn't figure out why.

"We've bumped up the security. She'll be safe, and you two can remain here in your room without worrying," Nathan pressed.

"Added security? Why would we need..." I trailed off as the memories of the ring and Abner's note slammed into my brain.

Irrational fear knocked the wind from my lungs, and my heartbeat thundered faster and faster.

DANGER.

My internal warning system blared the warning in my mind.

DANGER.

VAMPIRES.

DANGER.

No, that was wrong. The vampires wouldn't hurt me. I might be at risk, but not from them. Logic warred against the instinct to survive that erupted inside me.

"Journee. You're safe!" Zyon's voice pierced the haze filling my mind.

VAMPIRES.

DANGER.

I closed my eyes, fighting to clear my chaotic brain.

"Is she okay?" Nathan asked.

My self-control slipped, and I shoved Zyon off me. My unexpected burst of strength caught him off guard, and he toppled off the bed.

One vamp down, one to go.

"What in heck—"

That was all Nathan got out before I slammed into his chest, knocking him off balance. Delivering a swift punch to his throat, I watched as the vampire dropped like a bag of bricks.

Fight.

Survive.

Instinct was in the driver's seat, and I was a passenger. Vaguely, I knew something was wrong and that the vampire I'd attacked didn't deserve it. Peering down at the gasping vampire, I wondered if I knew him. He seemed familiar.

Arms wrapped around me, yanking me hard against a warm body. I squirmed and kicked, but the vampire holding me didn't budge.

"Tumbleweed! You're going to hurt yourself!"

Lies. Vampires always lie.

I couldn't trust the male vampire, even if his touch and voice called to something deep in my soul.

"We aren't going to hurt you!" the male shouted.

The second male vampire had pushed himself into a

sitting position. He was watching me with a wariness that made part of me sad and the other half delighted.

I was powerful. He should fear me.

Okay. That was it. I'd officially lost my marbles.

"My love, I swear you are safe. Come back to me." The vampire behind me pressed his lips to my neck as he pleaded with me.

I should have slammed my head into his, but instead, I tilted my head, giving the predator better access to the tender skin of my neck.

Closing my eyes, I breathed through the pain in my skull as I warred against instinct and my very soul.

"Mine," I whispered.

The vampire didn't hesitate. "Yes, I'm yours."

"You're not my enemy," I spoke the words out loud, trying to remind myself of the truth.

"No, I'm your soulmate. Your lover. Your monster." His lips trailed up my neck.

"Zyon." His name on my lips sent calm rushing through me.

Opening my eyes, I locked wide-eyed gazes with the second vampire. Guilt hit me like a sucker punch to the gut, instantly clearing the last of the mental fog. "Nathan!"

Zyon's arms remained locked around me, preventing me from rushing to check on his best friend.

Nathan turned to stare at Zyon. "She's a—"

"We don't know that!" Zyon snarled.

"Uh." Nathan's brow furrowed, and he slowly pushed to his feet. "Yeah, bro. We do know."

"Silence!" Zyon's order was sharp, but there was desperation beneath it. "It's impossible."

"I know what I just witnessed." Nathan eased away from us, but I couldn't tell if it was Zyon or myself that was making him uncomfortable. He froze, his eyes widening. "Was she attacking you this morning when I walked in on you two?"

Zyon's silence rang loud in the room, answering Nathan's question.

"She was trying to kill you." Nathan's voice rose in panic.

My muscles went slack. I'd tried to kill him?

"It's not her fault. She didn't know what she was doing," Zyon whispered, placing a gentle kiss on my neck.

Nathan looked at me, pity, worry, and sorrow swirling in his eyes. "We know that, but instincts are strong. You might as well have brought a hellhound into the castle and told everyone it's a golden retriever."

I dropped my eyes to the floor, unable to look at Nathan. "What's wrong with me?"

"Nothing." Zyon rumbled.

I tried to pull away from Zyon, but he held me tight. "Tell me the truth, Zyon."

When my soulmate said nothing, I looked at Nathan. "What am I?"

Nathan's eyes shimmered, "You're a Hunter."

"A Hunter?" The word stirred a memory in my mind, but I couldn't quite grasp it. "Like a deer hunter? I've never hunted for anything in my life!"

Nathan pointedly avoided my gaze.

Zyon stepped backward until he could sit on the bed and pull me onto his lap.

"No." Zyon sighed. "Nathan's talking about vampire hunters. They are a paranormal species with special abilities that make them efficient at killing vampires. They claim they are protecting humans, but even after vampires stopped killing humans and created agreements with human leaders, they were still killing us."

"How have I never heard of Hunters? Surely they would have been mentioned in the history books."

Nathan sagged onto an armchair, shaking his head. "For many years, the Hunters were the secret weapon of the human governments. They have always been good about hiding in plain sight and wiping away proof of their existence."

"There is a species out there hunting vampires, and you guys didn't think that was important to tell me?" My mind was reeling. Every time I thought I'd gotten my feet under me, the rug was pulled out from beneath me.

"No. Well, yes." Zyon struggled with his words. "Several decades ago, vampires stopped being killed by Hunters. We didn't know if the species had died out or if they'd finally realized vampires were no longer a risk to human lives and had retired."

The memory I'd been chasing came back to me, causing my lungs to seize up. "During the attack, you called Abner a Hunter. He's not human?"

Sorrow was etched on Zyon's face. "Abner was—is—a Hunter."

My insides felt like a plate-glass window that was slowly shattering into a million tiny pieces.

If Abner wasn't human, then I was in far more danger than I'd known. And not just me, but Zyon and the rest of the vampires were in danger too.

CHAPTER 8

journee

"Are you.... sure?" My words came out broken.

"Yes, I'm sure that Abner is a Hunter." Zyon brushed his finger against my cheek. "I'm not sure that you're a Hunter. You have some signs, but you're also missing several important ones."

"Bro! You can't tell me you didn't see her eyes!" Nathan sat up and leaned toward Zyon. "It makes so much sense looking back. Remember that first night at the restaurant, how she blurred across the room as fast as a vampire? And when she nearly hit me with that shard of glass after Abner's attack, her eyes were covered!"

Bile rose in my throat. I was going to be sick. As much as I wanted to deny it, Nathan was making sense.

Desperate to find some reason why it couldn't be the truth, I asked, "But why does my body warn me that vampires are dangerous? Why am I so scared of vampires that I can't be around them without sweating and hiccupping? If I were a Hunter, shouldn't I want to seek out vampires instead of going out of my way to avoid them?"

"And that is why I don't know for sure that you're a Hunter. You shouldn't have been able to be around so many vampires without snapping."

"She snapped on you this morning and again on both of us just now," Nathan pointed out.

"And both times, she was terrified for her life," Zyon snarled, his arms tightening around me. "This morning, her heart stopped. I thought I killed her! When she came to, she was confused."

"And just now?" Nathan's voice rose.

"She just found a threatening gift left by her stalker, who was supposed to be dead!" Zyon roared.

I laid my cheek against his heaving chest, hoping to calm him. "Zyon, it's not Nathan's fault. He's worried, and I just tried to attack him."

Both men remained quiet, giving me time to sort through my chaotic thoughts. "Nathan, you said it was dangerous to have me here. I can assure you I don't want to hurt any of you. If I'd wanted to, there've been plenty of opportunities."

Zyon was the one to speak first. "Because Hunters are driven to kill. They despise us for our bloodlust, but they are worse. By targeting vampires, they have been able to satisfy their craving for murder without dealing with the consequences of killing humans. By portraying us as evil creatures who can't control our impulses, they got the green light to hunt vampires and can even feel self-righteous about it."

"That's vile!" I clutched my throat and stared in horror at my soulmate's face. "How can any species be so cruel?"

Zyon shrugged. "I don't understand it either, Tumbleweed."

My eyes widened. "Zyon! We bound our souls together before you found out what I might be. Now you can't ever be free of me."

Zyon's reaction was unexpected.

His laughter rang through the room. "Silly Irenvyth, I would've bound our souls together even if I had known. We belong to each other forever, and this knowledge changes nothing."

Tears blurred my vision, and cool relief flooded my aching chest. Zyon still wanted me to be his.

"Has a vampire and a Hunter ever been soulmates?" Surely we weren't the only pair of star-crossed lovers, right?

Nathan snorted. "Not a chance. Hunters kill first and ask questions later."

I rubbed my forehead, trying to stave off a headache I could feel brewing. "So what's wrong with me? Am I just a terrible Hunter?"

"My best guess is you are a half-breed or part human and part Hunter. It would explain your minimal abilities and your lack of scent," Zyon answered instantly, showing he'd given this a lot of thought.

Nathan chewed his bottom lip, considering other possibilities. "You could also be from a weaker bloodline. Vampires still don't know too much about Hunters, but we do know there were several bloodlines. Each bloodline varied in strength and ability."

"But we don't know how many bloodlines are still in existence and how many are extinct." Zyon played with my hair. "This morning, I warned the guards and the queen that at least one Hunter was in the area and still eager to kill. For now, that is all we can do."

"Do you think you two could help me learn to control my impulses? You had to learn to control your bloodlust, so maybe I can learn too?" It was the only way I could see my life with Zyon working out. I'd never forgive myself if I hurt him.

"Of course. You have my full support!" Zyon kissed my forehead.

Nathan hesitated. "If the queen or any of the guards find out—"

"I'm ordering you to keep quiet about this. Tell no one." The force behind the order would have a weaker man on his knees, but Nathan remained standing. Zyon's voice dropped to a near plea for Nathan to understand. "She's my Irenvyth. Not a killer."

"I hope you're correct." Nathan shook his head, and it was clear he didn't actually think it would end well. "Out of respect for our friendship, I'll say nothing. I hope you two can find a way to sort this out. Between her not being human and you being whatever flying-demon-bat-thing you are, this seems like a ticking time bomb."

"We'll work through this. I've controlled my monster for centuries, and I can help Journee control hers."

Nathan strolled toward the door, then stopped, his hand on the doorknob. Glancing over his shoulder, his eyes bore into mine. "Journee, I want you to remember you're my friend, too. Whether you are a human or a Hunter doesn't change that. But if you're secretly a clown, I'm out. Those things are creepy as crap."

He left the room, and I dissolved into tears. Nathan might still be my friend, but he was right to be worried for all of us.

I wiggled from Zyon's arms. "I should leave the castle before I hurt someone."

"Journee, we don't even know for sure that you're a Hunter. You smell human, while Hunters have a unique scent." Zyon reached for me, but I evaded him.

"You said Abner masked his scent, so it is possible to mask a scent, right?"

At the mention of Abner's name, a muscle in Zyon's jaw twitched. "Abner was masking his scent, and that cannot be maintained long-term. You couldn't have managed to mask your scent for such an extended period of time."

He sounded so confident that hope bubbled in my chest. Maybe I wasn't a vampire killing machine. After all, I'd spent my life trying to avoid them rather than track them down. That had to be a good sign.

I sagged onto the bed. "But then, what's wrong with me? Why have I gone bat-crap crazy on you twice?"

"When we met, you were petrified around vampires. Perhaps that, combined with your concussion, stress, and exhaustion, has your fight-or-flight instinct in crisis mode?" Zyon kneeled in front of me, gathering my hands in his.

I liked that idea better than finding out I wasn't human.

"While you were sleeping, I arranged for additional security around the castle perimeter. The guards will also increase security in this part of the castle. If he gets in again, he won't escape alive."

I nodded, but deep down, I worried we wouldn't be able to stop him. He'd managed to survive certain death once, and now he'd snuck in and out of the prince's private chambers in the castle.

Abner seemed to bend the rules of what was possible, and that left me incredibly anxious. And if he was a Hunter, why was he so focused on me rather than killing Zyon?

"Would you like me to run you a bath?" Zyon bit his bottom lip, the tip of a sharp fang flashing.

My stomach fluttered in response. Not in fear, but in lust. How was he so effortlessly sexy?

"Journee..." Zyon hummed, his eyes glowing. Before I could stop him, he'd pulled my thighs apart and leaned down to take a deep breath. "You smell delicious."

We never did make it to the bath that night.

CHAPTER 9

journee

"Just think, only one more dinner to go after this party, and we are finished with the queen's requirements," Zyon leaned down to whisper in my ear.

We were walking through the castle's garden as guests milled around us. Instead of a breakfast social event, the queen had opted for a brunch in the garden.

Being outside versus crammed in a room with so many vampires made me far less anxious, and I was actually enjoying myself. "I could live out here! It's so beautiful!"

Zyon chuckled. "I am willing to live anywhere you wish on this earth, but I do require a house."

I sighed as though disappointed. "Fine, I guess a house would be acceptable. But only if you insist."

Zyon pinched my butt, and I squeaked in surprise, quickly checking to see if anyone had noticed. No one was paying me any attention because their eyes were all staring longingly into Zyon's face.

"You have quite the effect on the ladies, Casanova," I teased.

"Are they still staring?" Zyon whispered.

I snickered. "Yep. And most have some drool running down their chins now."

Zyon shuddered, pulling me closer.

Laughing, I tried to push him away. "Oh no! Those women are rabid! You aren't going to use me as a shield."

"I have a better idea." That was the only warning I got before Zyon spun me in his arms to face him.

His mouth met mine in a kiss that reminded me of our first kiss after I'd run into his arms. Zyon kissed me until my lungs burned with the need for oxygen. When he finally released me, I blinked, trying to clear the desire I knew was showing in my eyes.

"Zyon! We're not supposed to be acting like a couple." I hissed the reminder.

"Journee, I don't care what the rest of the world thinks. My grandmother is lucky I agreed to even attend these social events and that I'm waiting to announce our marriage. I want to shout it from the castle rooftop, but I'm resisting in order to keep the peace."

When he'd first told me I'd be attending these parties where women would be throwing themselves at my soul-mate, my heart had ached. He was mine, and I didn't want to share him, even if we were pretending.

I'd honestly worried if another woman touched him, I'd either want to throw down or throw up. Drama was something I'd tried to avoid my whole life, and I wasn't interested in adding it to my life now.

It turned out I shouldn't have worried. Zyon had shown up for each party as agreed, and he'd kept from publicly announcing our engagement. He'd also been a perfectly mannered gentleman.

But he had rebuffed or ignored every woman in attendance. Kelsey was the only vampiress he'd willingly spoken to, and that was because she was usually sitting on my other side.

I didn't need to worry about other woman drama because Zyon shut down every attempt to flirt or seduce him.

"What has you grinning like the cat who ate the canary?" Zyon smiled down at me, one eyebrow raised in suspicion.

My cheeks burned. "I was thinking about how you will shake hands, but you've threatened bodily violence on everyone else who has tried to touch you."

Zyon chuckled.

I began to giggle. "Their terrified faces are hilarious. They actually think you'd rip their arms off!"

My sexy prince stopped laughing and shot me a quizzical look. "Because I would. I'm yours, Tumbleweed. They have no right to touch what belongs to you, and I won't allow them to disrespect you."

It was the sweetest thing I'd ever heard—minus the bodily violence part. I blinked furiously, trying—but failing—to keep from crying.

"How did I get so lucky?" Forgetting where we were, I went up on my tiptoes. Throwing my arms around his neck, I covered his face and neck in kisses.

Zyon didn't hesitate to pull me tighter against him, grinning while trying to catch my lips. I teasingly kept him from it by placing kisses everywhere but on his mouth.

"It's a shame some vampires don't have enough self-respect to keep their feeders hidden behind closed doors."

"I've never seen such an embarrassment to the crown."

"He's always been a bit rebellious."

The whispers grew louder, and I tried to wiggle from Zyon's arms, but he refused to let me go.

"Let them talk," he growled, his hands sliding to my lower back.

"If you are going to talk behind their back, you are in a great position to kiss their butts! I bet you'd like that, though, wouldn't you, Beth?"

I recognized that last voice.

The Countess Du Pont had arrived.

"Hey, Ella! I see you're spreading more rumors about Journee! I'm delighted to see you've found a hobby where you spread something other than your legs!"

Zyon cackled in delight while I wheezed in shock, making a noise more like a rubber chicken than a human.

Nathan walked up beside us and slapped Zyon on the back. "We should have invited Kelsey back sooner. I've missed her."

"I bet you have." Zyon smirked, giving Nathan a knowing look.

Nathan good-naturedly mumbled something about Zyon being nice because Nathan knew too much.

When the haters wandered away, Kelsey grinned at me. "The two of you should either cool it or start charging. I've heard humans make good money making adult films. You should see how much I've made on OnlyFangs!"

My jaw dropped, and it was Nathan's turn to sound like a dying rubber chicken.

Kelsey rolled her eyes. "Stop clutching your pearls, Nathan. I swear I'm still a virgin. You'll be my first on our wedding night."

Nathan's eyes rolled to the back of his head, and he collapsed on the grass in a dead faint. At least, I thought he'd fainted.

"Is he okay?" I looked between the two vampires who stood over Nathan's prone body.

Zyon used his shoe to toe Nathan's side. "Yeah, he's fine."

"Good grief. It was a joke." Kelsey kneeled beside him, brushing her fingers through Nathan's hair. "You'd think he was still a virgin."

"You did mention having a wedding night with him," Zyon snickered.

Kelsey was quiet for so long I didn't think she would respond. When she finally spoke, the teasing note in her voice had turned serious. "I've waited so long for him to notice me. It seemed like I needed to try a more direct approach."

I patted her shoulder. "Why haven't either of you told each other how you feel?"

Kelsey's face brightened. "Do you think he likes me? Has he said something?"

"He's in love with you, and it's written on his face every time he looks at you!" Throwing up my hands, I spun on my heel and headed toward the open doorway that led to the bathroom. "Are all vampires dense?"

TWISTING the golden faucet over the sink basin, I washed my hands and dried them with a cream-colored paper towel embossed with the royal family's crest.

It felt weird and too expensive to throw away, but I couldn't carry it around with me. My cheeks burned just thinking of trying to explain to Zyon why I was carrying around trash.

Turning quickly, I searched for the trash can, only to bump into an antique side table. A beautiful blue and white porcelain vase wobbled and would have toppled off the table if I hadn't caught it.

I moved to sit it back on the shelf, but a voice I recognized came from the hall. Ella Wessex.

Not wanting to be alone in the bathroom with that horrid woman, I searched the room, looking for another exit.

There was a tiny door to the left, and praying it was a housekeeper's exit, I rushed to it. Flinging the door open, I rushed inside and pulled it closed behind me.

Was it a side exit? Nope.

It was a closet where the staff stored rolls of fluffy toilet paper, stacks of the too-pretty-to-use paper towels, and various other bathroom cleaning supplies.

Still clutching the vase in my hands, I spun around, intent on leaving the closet, but stopped. The closet door hadn't latched behind me, and there was a half-inch gap between the door and the frame where I could see into the rest of the bathroom.

I knew it was too late to make an escape when the door to the bathroom was shoved open, and three vampires walked in.

My choices were to wait for them to leave while I hid in the closet like some kind of weirdo, or reveal myself by coming out of the closet, which would also have them raising eyebrows.

There was no way for me to win in this situation. Through the small crack in the partially opened closet door, I watched them move in front of the mirror.

I didn't dare move or even breathe. If I was lucky, maybe the girls would be so caught up in their chattering they wouldn't notice the extra heartbeat in the room.

Stupid freaking vampire hearing.

The last thing I needed was for my chaotic heartbeat to draw the vampires' attention. Concentrating on my racing heartbeat, I was surprised when it began to slow little by little.

A familiar bubbling started in my stomach. As my chest spasmed, I slapped a hand over my mouth to silence the hiccup while still holding tight to the vase with the other hand.

They pulled various tubes of makeup, brushes, and powders from their diamond-studded and gemstone-bedazzled clutches and placed them on the large marble vanity.

It was astonishing how much could fit into those tiny little bags. I watched in awe as they continued to reach into the bags and pull out one item after another. Perhaps vampires did possess magic.

Or maybe they were going to break into a song about sugar being a good medicine. I'd actually really enjoy that. Sadly, I wasn't living in a musical.

"So, what do you think? Is he yummy, or is he yummy?" a familiar, red-haired vampire asked.

She was one of the vampiresses who'd confronted me after I left my appointment with Jamis. I think they called her Molly.

"He is as delicious as ever!" Ella licked her lips like a cat licking up cream.

"I'm telling you, Prince Zyon is like a fine wine. He gets better with every century," the third vampire, Beth, agreed.

Ella sniffed, annoyance flickering across her beautiful features. "Ladies, let's remember that Zyon belongs to me."

Unconcerned by her temper, Beth and Molly continued touching up their lipstick.

"Yeah, yeah, we know. We're here for moral support." Beth rolled her eyes.

Molly laughed. "And to be your wing-women."

"That's right." A calculating smirk slid across Ella's face. "You two are perfectly trained, and I'll remember your service when I'm queen."

Beth turned to face Ella. "And if he doesn't pick you, Ella? There's always the chance that could happen. Wouldn't it be better if one of us was picked?"

Ella giggled, playfully shoving Beth's shoulder. "You girls don't have a chance. Men can't resist me, and Zyon is no different."

Beth and Molly didn't seem too concerned by the insult, but the red-haired vampire's eyes narrowed ever-so-slightly. "I don't think any of us have a chance, as long as that human is hanging on his arm."

It took all my focus to keep my hiccups under control and my heart from galloping.

I wasn't going to panic...

I wasn't going to kill them...

"I don't know what the prince sees in her," Beth complained. "She's *human*."

Beth said *human* with the same tone of voice I suspected she would use when saying *cockroach*. Vampires might not be killing humans anymore, but it sure seemed like there were quite a few vampires who weren't fond of humans.

"She's probably just his new pet. You know vampire

men are prone to picking favorite feeders. It means nothing." Molly wiggled her eyebrows in Ella's direction. "Besides, are you going to tell me your male feeders are ugly?"

All three women burst into laughter.

"Of course not! Both of mine are athletes in the best shape of their life. But I'm not trashy enough to parade them around during events."

Beth tapped her chin with a long, tapered French manicured nail. "Maybe Zyon's doing it just to see how the vampire females will react?"

"Like a test! That makes sense." Molly nodded, using a brush to dab highlighter on the tip of her nose... then her chin, cheekbones, jawline... and basically everywhere else until she shined bright like a diamond.

It turned out that vampires did sparkle, or at least this one did. I had to bite my lip to keep from laughing at my lame joke.

"I hadn't thought of that!" Ella's face lit up—without the need for highlighter. "You might be right. Maybe he wants to see if the eligible females will be able to maintain control and decorum, even in uncomfortable and unusual situations."

"My thoughts exactly!" Beth used a tiny gold comb to brush her hair.

"So I should just pretend she doesn't exist?" Ella asked. For the first time, she sounded unsure.

"That's what I would do!" Molly's words were slightly muffled as she leaned toward the mirror to touch up her lips. "Besides, you aren't going to be able to touch her unless you can get her away from the castle guards and the witch Countess Du Pont. I would've taught the human a lesson on respect yesterday, but they interrupted."

"Then that's what I'll do. Treat her like she's nothing... because she *is* nothing. The prince won't even remember her once I'm in his bed."

They smiled at each other in the mirror, and a shiver trickled down my spine. There was nothing nice about these women.

After what felt like an eternity, they packed away their makeup and flounced out of the bathroom.

Fine. They didn't actually flounce, but in my head, they totally did.

I staggered out of the closet and leaned against the sink, using the quiet of the bathroom to calm the emotions warring in my chest.

It was exhausting being torn between the two halves of myself.

One side begging to flee and the other eager to fight.

Inner peace mostly restored, I moved to place the vase on the side table, but it was stuck to my hand.

Oh, for duck's sake!

Why couldn't I catch a break?

CHAPTER

10

zyon

I stood in the shadows of the hallway, watching as the three vampiresses left the bathroom. Still, Journee didn't come out.

A tendril of fear unfurled inside me. What if they'd hurt her?

I'd kill them. Then I'd bring them back, so I could kill them again.

Stepping from my hiding place, I stepped to the bathroom door and knocked. "Journee?"

The sound of sniffling and hiccups drifted through the door. Heart in my throat, I threw the door open to find Journee sitting on the floor. She was cuddling one of my grandmother's vases in one arm and clutched a paper towel in the other hand.

"Zyon!" she yelped, swiping at her tears and her nose with the paper towel.

I dropped to my knees in front of her. "Are you hurt? What's wrong, my love?"

"The paper towels were so pretty it was a waste to

throw them away, and then the vase almost fell, so I hid, but the vampires are jerks, my sweat feels sticky, and now I can't leave the bathroom." She cried harder.

I'd understood very little of what she'd said, but I hated seeing her upset. Sitting down on the bathroom floor, I pulled her onto my lap. I leaned my back against the sink and tucked her head under my chin.

She'd gone through chaos the past few days and proven she was such a strong woman. I think in her place, I'd have broken down far sooner.

Desperate to soothe my mate's heart, I began to hum a vampire lullaby my grandmother had sung to me as a child when I'd injured myself or felt lonely.

The door eased open, and my grandmother's head peeked inside. She took in my position on the floor, where I sat in my now rumpled suit, holding my sniffling mate.

I'd expected the queen to start barking commands and fussing about how anyone could have walked into the room and found the Crown Prince on the bathroom floor. But when I lifted my gaze in defiance, I was stunned to see her eyes soften so slightly that I might have imagined it.

Without saying a word, she twisted the lock on the door and pulled it closed behind her, giving me privacy with my Irenvyth.

Cradling Journee in my arms, I continued to hum.

Movement in the corner caught my attention. The shadows drifted across the floor as though they'd been called. Except I hadn't called them, and they didn't come to me.

Instead, they rolled around Journee, acting like worried puppies checking on their mistress. Journee lifted her hand, letting the shadows swirl between her fingers. There was a beautiful sense of irony that a Hunter was playing with shadows belonging to the abomination.

"Are you feeling better?" I kissed the top of her head, taking a discrete sniff of her scent.

"Yes. I'm sorry for the meltdown." Her voice was soft, but steady.

"There is nothing to be sorry for. You deserved a good cry."

"Zyon?"

"Yes?"

She blew out a heavy sigh. "I can't let go of the vase."

"If you want to keep it, I'll buy it from my grandmother. That isn't a problem." Personally, I thought the vase was ugly, but if Journee liked it, I'd buy a warehouse of them for her.

"I don't want to keep it!" She lowered her voice. "I think it is uglier than a monkey's armpit."

Laughter bubbled in my chest. "I couldn't agree more. So why are you snuggling it? Are you worried you hurt its feelings?"

Journee jerked her head to scowl up at me. "Ha-ha. No, I'm being literal. I can't put it down because it's stuck to my hand."

My stomach dropped. "Just like our hands at breakfast yesterday?"

Her jaw fell open. "I didn't think you realized. Why didn't you say something?"

How could I miss the fact our hands had been glued together? I hadn't said anything because I was trying to ignore the signs of her heritage.

I smiled. "Because I liked being glued to you, little mate."

Gently lifting the vase, I kissed the back of her hand, which was sealed tight against the porcelain. Ignoring her curious expression, I traced my tongue along the edge of her hand.

Little by little, her skin came unglued from the vase, and at last, I was able to set the eye-sore decor on the floor away from us.

"How'd you do that?" Journee twisted her wrist, looking at her palm.

I hesitated. It seemed wrong to teach a Hunter about their abilities—the abilities they used to kill vampires. But she wasn't a murderous Hunter. She was my Irenvyth.

"Hunters are able to produce a sticky substance from their palms. It is an ability they can use to slow down a vampire during an attack, giving them the needed advantage to kill the vampire." I hated the look of horror on my beautiful mate's face.

I'd seen several vampires lose a fight due to the Hunter's glue.

A Hunter could press their glue on a vampire's back, then slam them against a wall where the vampire would be stuck like a fly in a spider's web. Dripping some glue on the floor was enough to prevent a vampire from escaping by blurring away from the fight.

"I'm sorry, Zyon." Journee reached out to stroke my cheek but drew her hand away at the last moment.

Picking her hand up from where she'd tried to hide it beneath her skirt, I lifted it to my mouth and kissed it. "You're not a killer, Journee. There is nothing to be disgusted about when it comes to your body."

Journee's curiosity pushed her to ask more questions. "How did you dissolve the glue?"

"Hunters have magic which allows them to avoid being stuck in their glue. Vampires lack that skill, so over time, we figured out that saliva will break it down enough that we can free ourselves." I didn't tell her that the vampire who'd discovered the saliva trick had been about to chew his hand off in order to escape a Hunter's trap.

"Why do my palms only get sticky when I'm scared or nervous?" Journee traced the lines on her palm.

"I'm not sure, but I'm guessing it is one of your unique quirks? Maybe your body is doing it automatically for protection, but since you don't know how to control it, the glue is just a nuisance?" I suggested.

"That makes sense. I guess." Journee rubbed her palms one last time on her skirt, before standing. "We should go check on Nathan."

"I'm sure Countess Du Pont is taking care of him." Pushing to my feet, I tucked her dark hair behind her ear. "Do you want to tell me about what the 'jerk' vampires said about you?"

"It was the usual catty stuff. No biggie, I was overreacting." Journee avoided meeting my gaze. "Besides, it wasn't the stupid insults that upset me. I've heard that stuff before."

"Then what did they say that upset you? It will be good to know, so I can explain why I'm kicking them out of the castle." Lifting her chin, I searched her eyes for the truth.

"No! You can't do that! We are so close to completing the agreement you made with your grandmother. They'll be gone soon enough."

"What did they say, Tumbleweed?" I pressed.

Her cheeks bloomed with an adorable flush. "Ella talked about getting you in her bed."

I couldn't help it. I gagged.

Journee's eyes began to glow, but instead of the usual Hunter's green, they glowed a brilliant turquoise. "And part of me wanted to kill her."

The smart decision would've been to step away from her, but a perverse part of me loved knowing she felt jealous over me.

It meant she claimed me as hers.

"You never need to worry about another woman." I brushed my thumb across her bottom lip. "For however long I may live, I only want you."

"Show me." Journee caught my thumb between her teeth. Her eyes continued to glow, and the intoxicating fragrance of her arousal blossomed around us.

"Do you want to go back to our room—"

Journee pushed the thin straps of her dress off her

shoulders, letting it slip to the floor. She was naked other than her lacy thong.

I struggled to breathe as I drank in the sight of my soulmate's perfect body. Journee stepped forward, her fingers working my belt buckle to undo my pants. Within seconds, she'd freed my erection and kneeled in front of me.

My body twitched with anticipation, waiting for her next move. When her tongue darted out to tease the sensitive head of my cock, I hissed at the sensations surging up inside me.

"Journee," I moaned.

My fingers found their way into her silky hair, massaging her scalp while her tongue teased the tip of my erection.

"You don't have to do this. Let me pleasure you." I struggled to speak past the desire clogging my throat.

Her only response was to take me deep into her mouth.

"Ohhh," I groaned, my fingers tightening in her hair. "That feels…"

I was unable to speak as she slid my length in and out of her beautiful mouth. With each stroke, she took me deeper until I was hitting the back of her throat.

Journee reached up to touch my fingers in her hair, pressing them harder against her scalp. Using her hand, she guided my hand to show she wanted me to take control of the pace.

Satisfaction radiated from the monster locked inside me.

Tightening my grip on her hair, staying careful not to

hurt her, I guided her mouth down my length. Pulling free of her mouth, I thrust forward, burying myself deep.

"Such a beautiful pet."

Journee moaned around her mouthful of cock, the vibrations causing me to swell to the point of pain.

It was too much. There was no way I was going to last.

I held her head still. "Journee, we have to stop. I'm going to come."

"That's the goal." Her mouth enveloped me again, her tongue teasing and rubbing along my length.

"Journee—" I tried to protest, but it was hard to think when her throat was squeezing my cock.

Her fingers moved to the base of my erection, milking and massaging.

Looking in the large wall mirror over the vanity, I could see my naked soulmate on her knees in front of me, hungrily taking my length in her mouth.

It was incredibly erotic, and I made a mental note to return the favor in front of a mirror so she could experience the same.

My body tightened, warning that my orgasm was moments away. I tried to pull away to angle away from her. "I'm about to come."

"Good." Journee took me in her mouth again, refusing to allow me to pull away.

With one final thrust of my hips, I buried myself deep. Pleasure had me seeing stars as my cock jerked, and her throat worked not to choke.

Journee finally released me from her mouth and stood

slowly. When she met my eyes and licked her lips, I nearly came again.

How did I get so lucky?

My heart was completely lost to this woman.

Heaven help anyone who ever tried to take her from me.

CHAPTER 11

journee

Zyon had wanted to leave the party and go to his room, but I convinced him we needed to follow through with his agreement with the queen. Reluctantly, he followed me back outside.

"Stop looking so sulky," I teased.

"We could be having more fun in our room if you weren't so stubborn," Zyon growled against my ear.

I shivered in delight at his husky voice. "I promise we will later."

Kelsey appeared at my side and linked her arm through mine. "Oh, good! You two finished your adult nap time just in time to eat!"

My entire body blushed. Was it that obvious what we'd been doing?

"Don't look so embarrassed. Most of the people here think he was feeding from you. Only a few believe you two were polishing the porpoise."

I honestly wasn't sure which was worse and decided to pray for the ground to open and swallow me.

The earth must have been ignoring me, because there wasn't so much as a tremor beneath my feet.

"Come on, Nathan and I saved you a seat across from us." Kelsey led us through the maze of tables to one right smack in the middle of all the tables.

Every single set of eyes watched us—or, more accurately, watched Zyon. Fizz bubbled up in my throat, and I hiccupped. My chest muscles ached from the near-constant hiccups I'd experienced the past several days.

Just make it through today... I tried to give myself a mental pep talk.

The moment we took our seats at the table, the waitstaff hurried over with trays laden with food. I placed bacon-wrapped figs drizzled with maple syrup, a fresh cucumber salad, and two small finger sandwiches on my plate.

I had to give it to the castle chefs, they created magic in the kitchen. It almost made up for the company I had to deal with while eating.

Focusing on my adorable mini-sandwich, I tried to ignore the vampiresses who kept finding reasons to pass by our table just so they could try to catch Zyon's attention.

Zyon didn't even seem to notice their efforts, though. He was deep in a conversation about a vampire friend of Nathan's who was buying a circus while sneakily trying to slide his hand higher up my thigh beneath the table skirt without me catching on to his movement.

Which was laughable since my skin tingled and warmed every single time Zyon touched me. There was no way I'd miss my body's reaction to his skin brushing against mine.

"Prince Zyon, have you been on any trips recently?" a woman sitting a couple of seats down from us asked.

Zyon's fingers tightened imperceptibly on my thigh, but when he spoke, his voice was polite. "I visited Argentina a few months ago. Such a beautiful country."

She leaned on her hand, her eyes dreamy as he spoke. "It sounds amazing. I'm way past due for a vacation. Maybe you could give me some pointers on where to stay?"

Nathan took a sip of his drink. "Actually, I booked that trip. I'll have my assistant email you a list of suggestions, Tessa."

Realizing her attempt at getting closer to the prince had been thwarted, Tessa's face fell in disappointment. I felt bad for her until I remembered she wanted my man.

"Prince Zyon, there you are!" Ella sauntered up to our table, pushing between Zyon and my chairs. "The waiters told me my seat would be reserved here. I guess they must have forgotten."

Ella must have been taking the advice she'd received in the bathroom, because not once did she make eye contact with me. Snapping her fingers, she motioned for a confused waiter to bring her a chair.

Snatching the chair, she tried to push it between Zyon and my chair. Zyon put an end to her efforts when he rested his arm across the back of my chair, blocking her efforts.

Not willing to give up so easily, Ella shoved her seat into the only gap at the table... the space on my other side. This left me sandwiched between Zyon and Ella.

I didn't miss the way Kelsey used her cup to hide a

smile over my predicament. She'd pay for that sometime in the not-so-distant future.

Leaning her elbow on the table, Ella spent the next fifteen minutes trying to start a conversation with Zyon while ignoring me as though I was invisible.

I was tempted to act my shoe size rather than my actual age by making faces at Ella to see if she could resist acknowledging me. But I fought the urge and acted like the lady my mother had raised me to be.

Right up until Ella held out a bite of a cookie she wanted Zyon to try.

She wanted to feed my mate, and she had the actual freaking nerve to hold the food directly in front of my face.

Leaning forward quickly, I ate the bite of cookie from her hand. Before I could think my actions through, I turned and spat it delicately into my napkin.

Making a face as though it was the nastiest thing I'd ever tasted, I grabbed my throat and coughed. "I hate to be the one to tell you this, but I think your cookies are stale."

I only had myself to blame for what happened next.

A LOT HAPPENED ALL AT ONCE.

The entire length of the rectangular table gasped and fell silent.

Well, almost everyone was silent.

The Countess Du Pont shoved to her feet and began a slow clap while proudly telling the horrified vampiress sitting next to her, "That's my girl!"

"We're keeping her," Nathan wheezed between his loud guffaws.

In an instant, Ella's expression switched from sweet-as-pie as she made bedroom eyes at Zyon to a murderous rage as she finally acknowledged my existence.

In a fury-powered blur, Ella's hand darted out, raking me across the cheek with her sharp-tipped fingernails.

Adrenaline spiked through me, and the dark thing in my chest seeped through every muscle in my body.

Ella was moving at vampiric speed, but to me, she seemed to be moving in slow motion, like when you slow down a video to watch the weird faces someone makes frame by frame.

Or maybe I was the only one who did that for entertainment.

As the nails of Ella's right hand tore the skin across my cheek, her left hand gripped a butter knife from the table. Her arm arched through the air, moving toward my chest.

I should have moved, but I was in a trance. Would she actually follow through? Or would she realize the idiocy of killing me in front of so many witnesses and stop before the blade plunged into my chest?

Honestly, it was a dick move to use a dull blade to stab me.

I watched the knife with detached curiosity, confident I could move before she pierced my skin. Around the garden,

all the vampires were moving at the same speed as Ella—
which meant they were barely moving at all.

Kelsey was mid-leap as she jumped onto the table
toward me.

Nathan had lurched from his chair, sending it flying
back several feet as he reached across the table.

Turik was about ten feet away and blurring toward me
even as a throwing knife flew from his hand toward Ella's
back. She was a vampire, so it wouldn't kill her, but it
would hurt like Hades.

Most of the other vampires around the table were
scrambling away. Which was pretty smart thinking since I
doubted this was going to end in us braiding friendship
bracelets.

My gaze landed on the queen, who'd stood from her
chair, her face twisted in pain. I was the one being attacked,
so why would she look hurt?

Besides, if Ella killed me, that would make room for
Zyon to marry a more fitting bride. Wasn't that what she'd
wanted?

The one reaction I hadn't banked on was Zyon's.

He was faster than the other vampires, and although he
was still in slow motion, he was actually moving, while
everyone else was moving at a frame-by-frame rate.

The knife was an inch from my chest. I readied my
muscles to shift out of the way, only to be pulled backward.

Zyon's hiss was that of a viper warning of a death-
inducing strike.

His arm had dropped from the back of my chair to my

waist, jerking me back and away from the downward blade. At the same time, he lunged for her throat, knocking her from her chair.

Zyon was so focused on attacking my would-be murderer he'd put himself in the path of both the dull butter knife and Turik's far sharper blade that spun through the air.

Coming out of my stupor, I blurred forward, catching the dagger in midair. Using the blade's momentum, I spun it in my hand as though I'd done it a thousand times and slammed it down into the table.

While the rest of the vampires were moving too slowly to be able to process my speed, Zyon was the exception. His stunned, blood-red eyes locked with mine. That split second was all it took for the butter knife to pierce his shoulder.

"No!" I screamed, darting forward to squeeze between Zyon and Ella.

Yanking the knife from his shoulder, I flung it to the grass. My eyes locked on the trickle of blood visible through the tear in his shirt.

Without thinking, I leaned forward. My tongue licked along the torn skin.

I should've been grossed out, but the tiny drops of blood exploded like Pop Rock candy in my mouth, spreading cinnamon-spiced honey along my tongue. He tasted delicious.

Wow, my parents hadn't been joking when they warned me that I'd become like those I hung out with. I didn't think that I'd start liking blood just because I was in a castle full of vampires, but I guess you live and learn.

Zyon's gasp was followed by a feral growl as his muscles flexed.

He was about to shift in the middle of the party. I couldn't let that happen. He was larger than me, but the energy coursing through my body wasn't concerned.

"Hold on to me and start running!" I ordered, wrapping my arms around him.

Using my speed, I pushed both our bodies to blur at a speed that wasn't only impossible for a human, it was impossible for a vampire.

Like it or not, that left only one option.

I was a Hunter.

WE'D BARELY closed and locked the bedroom door before Zyon lost control and shifted to his monstrous vampiric form.

Standing to his full height, he slowly turned to face me. Zyon's wings unfurled with a sharp snap, and his gray skin glistened with sweat. His thin-slitted pupils locked onto me, and the double row of fangs caught the firelight in the room.

He looked ready to punish someone.

Bite me, I've been a bad girl. The unbidden thought popped into my mind.

"I'd be happy to." The monster in front of me licked his lips, and the rumbling bass of words seemed to stroke my skin.

I'd spoken out loud, but I couldn't work up any embarrassment... not when I was struggling to keep from throwing myself at him like a cat in heat.

"Before I make you come so hard you pass out, why did you lick my blood?" He took an intimidating step toward me.

A quick glance at his face was all I needed to see to let me know I'd broken an unspoken vampiric rule. But how was a girl supposed to learn all the do's and don'ts in under a week? They were expecting a lot from me.

Zyon's long-clawed finger reached out to touch my jaw, then slid down my neck and between my breasts. "Why did you taste my blood, little one?"

"I don't know," I panted. "Maybe I just wanted to lick you, so everyone would know you're mine?"

The monster barked a harsh laugh, his hand gently cupping my breast through my dress. "You can't be serious."

"I wasn't thinking clearly. But I remembered how your saliva healed me, and I wanted to try it on you." My words were barely audible, thanks to my desire making it hard to breathe.

"But I'm a vampire. Humans and Hunters lack healing

properties in their saliva. In fact, I've heard of humans getting infections from other humans' saliva."

My eyes moved to Zyon's shoulder. His perfectly tailored suit was torn, unable to adjust to the much larger body of the monster. The shirt hung off his body, giving me a clear view of the stab wound.

I gaped, and my stomach dropped. His shoulder was healed. And I don't mean it was nearly healed. No, the skin on his shoulder appeared as though it had never been injured, let alone pierced with a butter knife less than five minutes before.

How could that be?

"Vampire healing is crazy quick," I whispered in awe. "And you didn't even need to focus on healing it!"

Zyon stared at his skin. "I didn't heal it."

"But it's gone!" I pointed out the obvious.

"Yes, I can see that," Zyon muttered. "But I'm telling you, I'm not the one who healed it. That injury would have taken two or three hours to heal."

His piercing silver eyes bore into mine. "Your saliva healed me. But humans can't heal…"

"I'm not human." There was no sense trying to deny the truth.

His mouth dropped to mine, stopping when they were a hair's breadth apart. "It doesn't matter. Vampire. Human. Hunter. I don't care what you are. All that matters is you are mine."

"I love you," I whispered, but Zyon was too busy ripping the dress from my body to hear me.

CHAPTER 12

zyon

I was fighting against the need to rampage through the castle. My monster demanded the heads of every vampire who'd dared to even look the wrong way at our mate.

If it hadn't been for the stroke of her tongue lapping up my blood, and her hyper-speed getting us to my room within seconds, I would have shifted in the garden.

And I wouldn't have cared. I was ready to make it crystal clear that Journee was not to be touched, and anyone who went against my will wouldn't live to regret their decision.

My control was hanging by a single frayed thread.

"I love you."

Three little words.

It was those three little words that knocked my entire world off its axis, and the last of my control shredded… just like her dress under my claws.

I merged with the monster, allowing primal instinct and need to consume me.

"You should run." I felt the need to warn her, my words barely intelligible.

Her speed in the garden had been jaw-dropping and had made my speed seem slow. She might be able to outrun me.

The little minx wiggled out of the tattered dress, kicked off her shoes, and leaped into my arms. My waist in this form was too broad for her to wrap her legs around me, but she managed to hook them over my hips.

Cupping a hand under her rounded butt, I supported her weight and relished the heat I could feel radiating from beneath the lacy thong. Unable to resist, I ground my palm against her clit and growled in appreciation when she wiggled her hips and moaned toward the ceiling.

Her throat was displayed, and I sucked and kissed the column of her neck. When I moved to her mouth, the sweet scent of her blood tickled my nose.

Vision flickering, I took in the three dried lines of blood on my Irenvyth's cheeks. I'd been so lost in my rage, I'd only just noticed.

My body shook violently, forcing Journee to cling to me or slip from her perch. "Did she do that?"

I didn't need to clarify who *she* was. We both knew who I was talking about. Journee's back had been to me when Ella's arm had shot out. I'd seen her grab the knife, but I didn't know that she'd already made contact with my mate's skin.

The walls of my room cracked and popped as my rage

took on a life of its own. Curling my hand around Journee's waist, I tossed her to the bed.

"I'll be back." Blurring to the door, I was about to rip it open when Journee launched herself onto my back.

"No! You're going to stay here and do the monster mash with me!"

Reaching behind me, I dislodged my clingy mate. I tossed her across the room, careful to ensure she landed on the bed.

Her butt bounced once before blurred so fast she disappeared briefly before scaling my body. I grunted in surprise when Journee's glowing turquoise eyes appeared inches from mine.

"I'm not going to give up so easily," she snarled. "You're not leaving this room."

My monster didn't appreciate being told what to do, even if it was our soulmate giving the orders. "She must be punished."

Journee caught my large, gargoyle-like head in her hands, forcing me to look at her. "Ella doesn't matter right now. You can deal with her later."

Striding to the bed, I gently laid her down on the mattress. Journee grinned, thinking she'd won.

Leaning back, I quickly rolled her twice in the comforter, creating a Hunter burrito. Hoping it would slow her down, I blurred to the door.

Electricity crackled behind me and was quickly followed by Journee's weight settling on my shoulders. Her legs wrapped around my neck, and my body responded instantly to her soft skin brushing my neck and face.

"Bad vampire," she purred near my ear.

I'd show her a bad vampire.

Gripping her thighs, I spun her around on my shoulders. The new position had her slit against my mouth— something I took advantage of.

A flick of my claw took care of the lacey thong. I plunged my tongue inside her slick heat, using the extra length provided by this form to flick and stroke her in a way no human tongue could achieve.

"Zyon!" Journee's legs trembled around my neck, but she didn't try to escape my ravaging tongue.

My chest swelled with pride when her walls began to tighten within a minute of my tongue slipping inside her. She screamed, clinging to me as pleasure burst through her.

I'd slowly made my way to the couch, and she didn't seem to notice when I lowered her back down on the cushion. Slurping and lapping, I devoured every last drop of her sweet cream while she continued to tremble beneath me.

When I was sure she was lost in the fog of post-orgasmic bliss, I darted to the door. Yanking it open, I was surprised to find Journee standing in the hallway.

I yelped in shock. How'd she manage to blur past me? Realizing she was completely naked and anyone in the hall could see her, I yelped again and snatched her back inside the room.

Slamming the door with enough force to shake the

entire room, I bent to put my face near her flushed face, blowing out a harsh breath. "You're testing me, little mate."

I towered over her, a furious, winged, nine-foot-tall monster. Journee should have crumpled in fear, but she took a step closer. Tilting her head back, she flashed her teeth at me.

Was she insane? I was losing it, and she wanted to challenge me for dominance?

She wasn't going to win this one. Leaning down until our faces nearly touched, I bared my terrifying double row of dagger-sharp fangs.

Journee grabbed my face, going on tip-toe to press her lips to mine. Her tongue darted out, and before I could pull away, she ran it across my fangs.

The sweet taste of her blood exploded in my mouth, stealing every thought from my mind other than the need to give into my lust.

I'd told her to run, but she hadn't listened.

Grabbing her hips, I hauled her off her feet and skewered her on my hard length. I knew I should have given her time to adjust to my size, but I couldn't stop myself and her sweet pleas for more were like pouring gasoline on a fire.

Holding her hips, I lifted her, only to sheath myself deep. Faster and faster, I plunged into her tight body. The bloodlust was creating a tornado of need inside me, driving me to take what I needed from my mate.

There was a part of me that was terrified I'd injure her or terrify her to the point she couldn't bear to be with me, but the monstrous instincts were in control, and I could do nothing to douse the raw lust demanding release.

My eyes landed on the three red lines across her cheek, and anger flared. How had she gotten those? I felt like I should know, but the fog in my mind made it hard to locate the answer.

I flicked my tongue along her cheek, cleaning the shallow wounds and accelerating the healing process. At the touch of my tongue on her skin, Journee's walls tightened around my engorged cock.

Rumbling my approval over my mate's reaction, I curved my body so that I could continue pounding into her, but also had better access to her breasts. My tongue curled around the hardened peak of her nipple.

Journee arched her back, pushing her chest toward me. Happy to give her what she wanted, I licked and sucked her breasts. I delighted in how they'd grown heavy with her arousal.

"Zyon," she whimpered, her nails digging into my skin as her breath quickened with her impending climax.

Three more hard thrusts and she came apart, her tight channel trying to milk my cock. I fought the urge to join her in bliss. There was something else I wanted from my mate.

Her blood.

I flipped Journee over the cushioned back of the couch, giving myself a better position to claim her smaller body.

Her beautiful body was ready to be mounted.

Pressing my chest to her back, I nipped the skin of her neck, warning her of my intentions. Journee reached up and brushed her long hair off her neck. Turning her head, she offered her neck.

Looking back, I hated the way I'd clamped down on her neck and sucked like a wild animal. She was giving me something I never thought I'd experience in my life. The least I could do was make it good for her too.

But I was past any type of control. Reaching between my legs, I stroked the armor-like plates that lay just under my cock. I was beyond turned on. That combined with her blood running down my throat and her fragrant arousal heavy in the room, it didn't take much to stimulate the hidden appendage.

My monster's cock unfurled from beneath two of the protective scales and filled with blood. I guided the thinner and longer length around my already slick cock.

I pressed the tips of my cocks against her entrance. A sheen of sweat covered my skin as I fought the impulse to thrust hard and fast.

My body ached painfully, needing release before I burst. Rocking my hips, I pushed myself inside her delicious heat, one slow inch at a time.

With my heartbeat thundering in my ears, I could barely hear Journee's moans. Shifting my hips, I moved inside her and nearly passed out at the exquisite pleasure. How could something feel so good it hurt?

I'd never used the second cock during sex, and I hadn't been prepared for the way every sensation was being amplified. The second cock was growing hotter and rippling with my pumping blood.

"Zyonnnnn! I'm going to—"

I pulled my teeth from her skin, my body growing taut. "Come for me, pet."

My release hit me hard and refused to let me go as my cocks swelled, locking me inside my mate's body. My vision lit up in a firework show like nothing I'd ever witnessed.

Journee screamed until her throat was raw as orgasm after orgasm rocked her body, not giving her time to rest between each one.

When her scream cut off, and her body went limp under me, my heart lurched for a second, believing I'd killed her. The rise and fall of her chest calmed the terror clawing at my chest.

I braced myself on the couch, catching my breath. When my erections slipped free, I gathered her tenderly in my arms.

Lying down on the couch, I laid my mate on my chest. After tucking a mink throw blanket around her body, I allowed my heavy eyelids to drift closed.

I watched Journee stroll through the garden, her forest green tulle gown falling just below her knees and tiny gold stars scattered across the fabric glinting in the sunshine.

She wore a pair of simple gold flats that contrasted with the elegant heels the vampire women were wearing. I sighed. Heels would have displayed her legs far better. She'd foregone any makeup and opted for the natural look.

If she'd presented herself properly, she would have been the most beautiful female at the party. It was a shame she'd failed, but it was a mistake she wouldn't make once I began dressing her.

Under my care, Journee would learn to take pride in her appearance. She'd always be the best dressed in the room. My beautiful girl would never want me to be embarrassed having her on my arm.

Although, now that I thought about it, perhaps she'd purposely made herself less attractive. Yes. That made so much sense. Journee was rebelling in small ways, letting me know she only cared about pleasing me.

She brushed her hair behind her ear, and I focused on her fingers, searching for my gift. I was disappointed her hands were bare, but I wasn't surprised. It would have been risky for her to wear it and anger the prince.

Thanks to the chaos of so many visitors to the castle, it had been easy to sneak into the castle. After leaving the ring box, I hurried from the room to once again blend in with the staff.

Shifting positions in the tree, I ground my teeth together as white-hot agony seared my insides. I was supposed to be resting in bed, healing from what should've been fatal injuries.

Journee should appreciate my gift and my thoughtfulness in delivering it myself. It was important that my betrothed knew I hadn't given up on her. Our love was too strong to keep me away.

Now I was lurking near the castle, waiting to see with my own eyes that she was uninjured from the abomination's attack. Vampires were vicious beings, and every minute Journee was in that castle, she was at risk of being sucked dry.

No matter how sophisticated the vampires portrayed themselves to be, they were nothing more than bloodthirsty demons beneath their polished exteriors.

I wouldn't let them keep Journee as their pet.

My biggest concern was figuring out how to whisk her away from the castle before she sparked. Mari made it clear she hoped Journee would spark while surrounded by vampires, but that would mean certain death for my betrothed.

Journee would likely manage to kill several unsuspecting vampires before the demons ended her life. Even untrained Hunters from her line were efficient killers—but it would be a waste to exchange Journee's life for that of a handful of vampires.

As far as we knew, Journee was the only child produced by her parents, making her the last opportunity to continue her bloodline. She had to produce my heir before we risked sending her out on missions.

I refused to allow my seed to go to a bloodline that was unworthy of the honor.

Only Journee will do.

The fact I was out of bed and working to comfort and rescue my betrothed was a sign of my dedication and strength. Journee should be thankful I valued her so much.

Journee turned, a smile on her face. Irritation rippled through me. The marks of discipline I'd given her were completely healed. What a shame.

She'd needed to wear those marks for a while longer. How else would she learn from her mistakes? They were visible reminders of my love and my willingness to work through issues in our relationship.

Pride warred with my anger. For her to have healed so quickly, she must be an even more powerful Hunter than I had hoped.

But it was also a sign that her powers were rising, and

she would spark soon. I was running out of time to rescue her.

Journee looked out across the manicured gardens, pausing to stare at the stand of trees I was hiding in. Did she sense my presence?

"I'm here, my betrothed," I whispered, wishing I could rush to her side and teleport her away.

But I couldn't.

My strength was still drained from my injuries. There was no way I could teleport both of us to safety. For now, I'd have to be satisfied with watching and waiting.

The prince pulled her into his arms, kissing her mouth just as he had on the street.

"Push him away," I snarled.

Journee didn't struggle. She let him touch her.

Swallowing the bile in my throat, I reminded myself she was an untrained Hunter who was surrounded by vampires. By keeping the prince interested in her body, she was securing her safety and giving me time to come for her.

If only she hadn't decided to play this idiotic game the night she'd run into his arms. Everything had been perfect, and now it was ruined.

"She's a woman," I reminded myself, taking deep breaths to quiet my harsh breathing.

Journee was probably feeling lost without me nearby. After all, I'd spent months following her. My reassuring presence had given her peace and security.

And now she must feel utterly alone in the castle and unable to see me watching from the shadows.

"Be patient, Journee. It won't be much longer." I slid the flat blade of my knife against my mouth, imagining it was her lips I was caressing.

For over an hour, I observed the comings and goings in the garden. When Journee disappeared into the castle and Zyon followed after her a few minutes later, my anxiety spiked.

When they finally returned thirty minutes later, and she appeared unharmed, my muscles relaxed. They moved to sit at one of the dining tables.

A female vampire pushed her way between them, which I didn't mind since the prince was far too touchy with Journee.

I couldn't make out their words from this distance, but I did recognize the vampiress. Ella Wessex.

There was no denying the vampire was attractive, and I was surprised the prince continued to give his attention to the less flashy Journee while a woman straight from every male's wet dream was practically throwing herself at him.

Ella had been high on our list of targets for many years. But we'd decided that rather than killing her on the spot, we'd capture her to use as bait. Once we lured out the more dangerous and reclusive members of her family, we could slaughter them all.

But a plan of that complexity needed years to formulate, and we needed another elite Hunter in our ranks first. Journee would be that Hunter, but first, she needed to be trained and bent to my will.

Wessex was pressing herself into Journee's personal

space, and I chuckled at Journee's unbothered expression as she continued to nibble on her food. It was the type of confidence only an elite-born Hunter could maintain in the face of an unbalanced demon.

The female vampire leaned past Journee to offer the prince a piece of her food. Journee's patience snapped, and leaning forward, she ate the food being offered to the prince.

Journee made a disgusted face, and I wished I could've heard what she said to send the vampiress flying into a rage.

Ella screamed and flung out a hand. Her nails raked across Journee's cheek, leaving three thin trails of blood beading on my betrothed's skin.

It was the same cheek that had felt the kiss of my favorite blade in her apartment. This memory instantly had my body growing hard. It had been such an intimate, intoxicating moment shared between lovers.

The fog of lust combined with righteous anger began to consume me. How dare she injure Journee's creamy skin.

Journee would heal, but that wasn't the point. No one touched what was mine. Only I could give her the pleasure that came with the kiss of pain. This vampire had drawn blood that belonged to me, and that couldn't be overlooked.

When Ella grabbed a knife from the table, my muscles tensed, and I gathered my strength to rush to Journee's side.

In the blink of an eye, the prince grabbed Journee and blurred her inside. His speed was incredible, far faster than my eyes had been able to track. It was a reminder to watch my step when I next faced off with him.

I stared at the doorway the prince, and Journee had disappeared through and wished I could see if she was okay.

Was she allowing the abomination to comfort her after Ella's attack? It was normal for females to crave reassurance from strong males in times of stress, but I couldn't help the disgust that roiled in my stomach at the thought of his skin touching hers.

My attention turned back to the out-of-control female vampire as she continued to scream after the prince. The royal guards and the prince's best friend quickly restrained her. Her shouts grew louder, until, even from a distance, I could hear her words.

"I will kill you! Do you hear me, human?"

That wouldn't do.

Cold fury turned my blood to ice. I'd been planning to return to headquarters to rest, but it seemed my work at the castle wasn't finished.

CHAPTER 14

journee

"T"he entire castle is buzzing with the rumor that you and the prince are a thing." Kelsey grinned at me, a wicked gleam in her eyes. "After he whisked you away and then neither of you showed up for dinner, most of the ladies here realized they didn't have a chance. I'm surprised we haven't floated away with the number of tears that have been shed since last night."

I said nothing, remaining motionless as Kelsey fussed with my makeup.

"Oh, come on! I can tell you're gloating on the inside!" She giggled when she caught my tiny smirk.

"I didn't realize how much I enjoy the sound of grown vampires throwing tantrums while sipping my morning coffee. In fact, there's a rumor that Ella hasn't even shown her face since the garden party." Kelsey dropped her voice. "Probably because she's too busy throwing a tantrum over the way the prince protected you yesterday."

I hated what went down at the luncheon, but I didn't

regret what happened afterward. By preventing Zyon from hunting Ella down, I'd aroused something feral in him.

He hadn't been lying when he told me he was equipped with two silent flutes, and they'd left me thoroughly satisfied and struggling to walk. I wondered how long I had to wait before we could do it again.

"Are you even listening to me? Or are you going to keep reliving the memories of him spelunking in your cave of wonders yesterday?" Kelsey tickled my nose with a makeup brush.

"What?! I wasn't thinking—"

"Lies! You were practically glowing just now. Plus, I didn't miss your bow-legged stride. You were riding something pretty hard…"

We burst into giggles.

When we'd settled down, I circled back to our previous conversation. "Ella really has it out for me."

Kelsey snorted. "That's putting it mildly! She was screaming about how she was going to kill you the entire time Nathan dragged her away! Look up, Jo."

I looked to the ceiling, holding perfectly still while Kelsey swiped mascara on my lashes, being careful not to stab me.

The queen had planned a spectacular dinner for this evening. It was the only event being held today. She'd asked that Zyon and I keep our engagement a secret for two days and attend the social events she'd put together.

On the third day, Zyon was free to announce our relationship. He would also be free to decline invitations to social events, and he wouldn't be required to help entertain the castle's guests.

We'd spent a wonderful day relaxing in bed, eating snacks… and each other's bodies. For the first time since I'd run from Abner, I felt rested, and I was even looking forward to this evening.

"So, is Zyon going to make the announcement tonight?" Kelsey's eyes twinkled, and a knowing smile curved her lips.

"What announcement?" I tried to look innocent, but she wasn't buying what I was selling.

"That you two are madly in love and are going to get married and live happily ever after! *Duh*." She flicked her hair over her shoulder, doing her best valley girl impression.

I couldn't hide my snicker.

Kelsey dropped onto one of the vanity seats. "Come on! We're going to be best friends, which means no secrets."

I raised a brow. "You've already planned this out?"

"Of course I did. I need a reason to stay here, and you need a female friend who doesn't want to suck your blood or stab you with butter knives."

I squinted at her, trying to figure out her ulterior motive. "So you're using me?"

Kelsey beamed. "Of course! But isn't that what friends are for?"

How was I supposed to know? It wasn't like I'd ever had one of those.

"Plus, you need more friends your age." She picked up an eyeshadow palette.

"My age?" I gave a strangled laugh. "You are probably old enough to be my great-great-great-great—"

"Shut up!" She playfully shushed me. "I'm a lot younger than most of the old vamps haunting this castle. You're lucky to have me."

I couldn't deny that it would be nice to have her nearby. Especially since most of the other female vampires I'd met seemed to want to kill me.

"That's nice of you." It was my turn to tease her. "But are you sure you want to stay here because of me? Or is it so you can get closer to Nathan?"

Her brows rose, and her pale cheeks turned pink.

Busted!

I rolled my eyes. "A better question is, how long before you two make it official? He can't stop making lovey-dovey faces as it is."

Her eyes lit up. "He looks at me?"

"*Duh.*" I flicked my hair, mimicking her.

"Do you think I really have a chance with him?" Her tone was so hopeful I nearly marched her straight to his room to make them spill their feelings.

I smiled at her. "I'd say you have more than a chance."

Kelsey didn't say a word, but spun around to face the mirror and began to frantically touch up her makeup.

Glancing in the mirror, I found that only my bottom lip had lipstick, and one eye was still missing the black, winged eyeliner.

"Um, Kels? Are you gonna leave me like this?"

"Stop worrying! You look perfect!" she answered without glancing my way.

Shaking my head at young—er, old—love, I tried to finish my makeup myself.

A knock sounded on the door, and I opened it to find Turik standing in the hallway.

The guard bowed. "Good evening, Miss Journee. The queen has requested a meeting with you, and I'm to escort you to her."

I shot a panicked look at Kelsey.

"Don't look at me for help!" she hissed, throwing her hands up. "I'm headed to the ballroom to get a glass of champagne so I can start this evening off right."

"And so you can look for Nathan," I added, not bothering to hide the snark in my voice.

She grabbed her clutch and pushed past us. "Well, of course! I don't want to die an old maid."

My laughter echoed down the hall after her. "You're immortal, and you're already old."

Instead of replying, Kelsey waved at me over her shoulder… with one finger.

"She has a kind heart," Turik observed.

"You're a terrible judge of character," I teased. "Nathan's life will never be boring."

Turik chuckled. "If they ever work up the courage to express their feelings. I've known the Countess Du Pont since she was a youngster. Back then, she'd follow after

Nathan like a lost puppy. That poor girl has waited years for Nathan to notice her."

"Maybe he needs a push." I paused. "Or a shove."

"Or a hard smack to the back of his head," Turik suggested.

I laughed. "That would probably work, too."

Taking his offered arm, I closed the door behind me. "All right. Lead me to my execution—I mean, my meeting with the queen."

"It won't be that bad," Turik assured me. "Probably."

I'D EXPECTED to be taken to the queen's throne room, but Turik guided me to her sitting room in her wing of the castle.

He raised his hand to knock, but the queen swung the door open before his knuckles could connect with the wood.

"That took you long enough," she huffed. "It's not every day someone has the gall to keep me waiting."

Well, this meeting was off to a wonderful start. "I'm sorry, I didn't realize—"

"Oh, hush. Come in." Taking my elbow, the queen pulled me inside.

Unsure whether he should leave me, Turik shifted from foot to foot in the doorway.

"I'm not going to eat her, Turik. My grandson would have my head if I attempted it. Could you go supervise our guests and ensure they remain civil? I swear it's like we're babysitting children. Back in my day, manners and decorum meant something." The queen waved him away, and Turik closed the door as he left.

I bit the inside of my cheek to keep from snickering. It was hilarious to listen to this elegant woman, who didn't appear to be much older than thirty, reminiscing about things 'back in her day.'

Logically, I knew she was a lot older, but the incongruity between her words and her appearance was beyond comical.

"Have a seat." The queen waved me toward one of the large armchairs near a stained glass window before settling herself in a matching chair across from mine.

I sat stiffly, fighting the urge to white knuckle the arms of my chair. She claimed I was safe, but I worried that at any moment, she'd fly at my throat like she had during our first meeting.

My stomach began to churn with a familiar fizziness. Holding my breath, I hoped to stop the hiccups before they started.

"You look as though you're expecting me to yell 'off with your head' at any moment. The amount of anxiety rolling off you is making me nervous." The queen tapped her fingers on the arm of her chair. "Contrary to what you believe, I love my grandson. Which is why I've brought you here."

Oh, crap! I've seen this movie before. This is the part where a well-meaning parent—or grandparent—lists the many reasons I wasn't good enough for her grandson. By breaking my heart and tearing down my self-esteem, to the point I was a crying mess, I'd rush to my room, pack my bags, and using the large check that she'd given me, I'd disappear under a new identity. Not today, Satan. It wasn't happening.

The queen burst into laughter, holding her sides as she struggled to catch her breath.

It took several horrifyingly long seconds to realize I'd said every bit of that out loud. Even the Satan part.

"I'm sorry," I stammered. "I didn't mean that. Well, actually, I did mean that. But I didn't mean to say it out loud—"

"Stop rambling." The queen leaned back in her chair, still chuckling quietly. "And to be honest with you, I had considered that very plan of action but changed my mind."

"Why?" my mouth asked before my brain could close it.

"Because vampires live a very long time, and my grandson would spend the next seventy years or so searching for you. He is relentless when he wants something." Her calculating eyes softened. "If you truly are his Irenvyth, it would be cruel to separate you two."

Sagging back into my chair, I sighed in relief. I'd come here expecting to be berated, threatened, and possibly beheaded, but I hadn't thought this was a possible outcome.

"I won't lie to you. It frustrates me to no end that you

are human. That will eventually create a messy situation. You will die, and I will be left with a heartbroken grandson. Zyon doesn't heal easily, and it will take several centuries after your death for him to pull himself together again." She sighed. "But it cannot be helped now. Who knows? Perhaps having you as our princess will even help strengthen our reputation among humans. As you know, we have quite a lot of work to do to fix our infamous reputation."

The queen smiled, flashing her sharp fangs.

I gave a nervous laugh, unsure what response I was supposed to give.

The queen laced her fingers together, resting them on her knee. "One thing has surprised me."

"What's that?" I asked when she didn't continue.

"I've been watching the young vampiresses who are vying for my grandson's attention. They are obnoxious! It's no wonder my grandson has adamantly refused marriage time and time again, if this is the best we had to offer him."

I stayed quiet, not sure where this was going. I'd been threatened, scratched, confronted, insulted, and nearly stabbed by the vampiresses, so I didn't disagree with her assessment.

"You should never play poker, child. Your face is far too easy to read. And yes, I've observed the way many of the girls have interacted with you. My staff and I have witnessed things my grandson has not. And you deserve an apology."

CHAPTER 15

journee

I had to be hearing things.

How could the angry woman who'd nearly choked me to death, and insulted me for being a human, be offering me an apology?

"I'm afraid you haven't been shown a very good side of vampiric society. And I can admit I tend to be a little crazy when it comes to my grandson."

A little? The woman had threatened to rip my throat out. But I didn't think this was the right time to remind her of that.

"The fact that you are still at my grandson's side, despite how you've been treated, is a testament to how strongly you feel about him."

The queen gave me a gentle smile. "I feared you were one of the vampire groupies who follow my grandson around. But I had my team research you, and they found you rather boring, dear. You've never shown any interest in vampires, and you barely even passed the required vampire school courses. This leaves me with one question. Why would someone who is so terrified of vampires want to stay in the castle surrounded by vampires? Many of whom would love to make you disappear to increase their chances with the prince? And yes, I am aware of your fear."

She waved a hand in my direction. "Even now, you're turning blue as you try not to hiccup. The only answer I can come up with is that you truly do want to be with my grandson. Is that the truth?"

"I love Zyon with all my heart," I answered without hesitation.

The queen studied me, her cold eyes searching my face for any sign of deception or manipulation.

She wouldn't find it.

My life was a hot freaking mess, but there was one thing I was absolutely sure of. And that was my love for Zyon.

"Can you feel the soulmate bond?" Curiosity flitted across her face.

"I can, although not as strongly as Zyon. I'm pulled toward him, even back when I was afraid. The bond reassures me that I'm safe with him."

"I'm happy to hear that. It's been a long time since I've seen my grandson this happy." Tears shimmered in the queen's eyes. Or maybe I was imagining things. "I know Zyon intends to announce your engagement this evening, and I wanted to tell you I accept his decision."

I swallowed hard. "Thank you."

"It's hard to teach an old dog new tricks, so I'm unsure if I'll ever be completely comfortable having a human in the family. But I want you to know that you will have the protection of the crown. You won't be at risk from me or anyone in my court. Nor will I allow anyone to disrespect you in my presence."

It was more than I'd expected or could have hoped for based on my past experience with the queen. I thought I'd be spending the rest of my life worried she would pop out of a dark corner and snap my neck like a twig.

"I appreciate that." I wanted to slap myself for the stiff reply, but how did you respond when someone tells you they won't try to kill you anymore?

"Thank you for your patience these past two days. When my husband was alive, I wanted to kill any female who so much as glanced in his direction. It had to be torturous for you to watch females throw themselves at your soulmate. You showed far more decorum than I could have managed." The queen shot me a conspiratory smirk. "Frankly, I probably would've thrown several of them off a balcony at this point. And if you choose to do so, I'll happily look the other way. This kingdom could do with a few less of these brainless idiots."

A grandfather clock in the corner of the room chimed, and I nearly leaped from my seat.

"It looks like you had better head to the dining room before my grandson storms in here looking for you. Hopefully, our talk has settled some of your fears about being around me."

"Actually, I believe it has helped." I stood and gave a weird half-bow, half-curtsy.

The queen quickly covered her mouth, but not quick

enough to stifle her snort. "Please don't ever do that again. It's going to take a lot of work to get you ready for life as a royal. Who knows, though? It could take a while, but we might even become friends before you grow old."

"Thanks. I guess?" I was unsure if she'd just complimented me or insulted me.

"Go wait in the hall while I gather my things. We won't enter the room at the same time since you'll enter with Zyon. But I will walk with you. My presence should help to make it clear that you aren't to be touched."

STEPPING OUT INTO THE HALL, I gently closed the door behind me. Leaning against the wall, I watched the staff as they hurried back and forth. They carried shining platters filled with food that looked so perfect it could be fake.

Three sharply dressed waiters scurried past me, each carrying trays nearly three feet wide. Each tray was covered in delicate champagne flutes.

A fourth server rushed behind them, carrying fresh table linens and napkins in a stack so tall she couldn't see where she was even going. Which explained why she barreled into me.

"Ompf!" The air was knocked from my lungs, and static electricity popped between us. With effort, I managed to wheeze, "Are you okay?"

The woman quickly caught her balance and bent to gather the fabric that had toppled off her stack.

"My apologies, miss." She straightened, making eye contact for the first time. Her next words poured over me like a bucket of ice. "I didn't expect to see a Hunter in the castle."

Surely, I'd misheard her.

I gave a weak smile. "Pardon me?"

"You heard me, Huntress."

I'd just learned I was a Hunter, so how could this woman know what I was? "I think you have the wrong person."

"I definitely have the right person, and I can tell by the look in your eyes it didn't surprise you to be called a Hunter," she hissed, taking a step closer to me.

My legs wobbled, and I clung to the wall for support. "I don't know what you're talking about."

Reaching out her hand, she pressed it against my chest. A green glow appeared beneath her palm, heating my skin through my shirt.

Calling on my inner strength, I batted her hand away. "Stop that! What are you doing?"

She must have gotten whatever information she'd been seeking because a wide smile split her face. "You haven't fully sparked. That means you aren't a traitor living among vampires. You're simply an idiot among vampires. There's hope for you yet."

I began to hiccup as fear and confusion churned in my chest. "What are you talking about? How would I be a traitor? And what does *sparked* mean? How much have you drunk today?"

The woman tidied the stack of fabric in her arms as best she could. All the while, she kept that infuriating, secretive grin on her face. "If I answered all of those questions, I'd ruin the surprise. Go have fun at your party, and be sure to stay close to the royal family."

Before I could say anything else, the queen stepped into the hallway, and the weird housekeeper scurried away.

I needed to find Zyon. Maybe he could explain how a stranger could know I was a Hunter. Was I wearing a sign now?

Bracing myself, I turned to the queen, half expecting her to scream that I was a Hunter as well.

But she didn't. She merely tilted her head in acknowledgment and strode down the hall, her spiked heels clicking against the polished marble floor.

CHAPTER
16

journee

I followed after the queen. My mind was reeling, and a migraine had started forming behind my eyes.

As we neared the grand ballroom, I spotted Zyon and Turik. The queen motioned in their direction. "Zyon is waiting for you to make your first formal entrance as a couple."

She took a step away, then halted. "And Journee? Take care of his heart."

With that, she disappeared around a corner to make her own appearance. Making my way to Zyon's side, he led me toward the top of the sprawling staircase that led down into the ballroom.

We waited in the shadows as trumpets sounded and the queen's arrival was announced. With an ease that came from many years of practice, she descended the stairs to the eager applause of the gathered vampiric guests.

My internal warning system had been quieter these past two days, but that didn't mean it was silent. I fought to ignore my rising panic. The last thing I needed was to glue my hand to the banister accidentally or hiccup like I was tipsy the entire way down the stairs.

"Journee?" Zyon turned me in his arms to face him.

"Yes?" I focused on the liquid silver of his eyes and the way the light glinted off his pale hair, creating an almost angelic glow around him.

His fingers caressed my cheek. "I love you too."

My heart stopped, and I stammered. "Y-you... heard?"

"It was the most beautiful thing I've ever heard. It rocked my world, and I lost control before I could tell you." Before I could find the words I needed to respond, Zyon took my hand. Stepping from the shadows, he led me to the top of the staircase.

A sea of faces looked up at us, and the room fell completely silent.

Releasing my hand, he took a step away from me. My confusion blossomed into joy when Zyon kneeled in front of me.

"Journee Elsher, I have lived for centuries, but I wasn't truly alive until you tumbled into my life. I love you, my beautiful Irenvyth. Will you please do me the honor of marrying me, so I can claim the title of your husband?"

Zyon held up a black velvet box. Opening it, he revealed a diamond ring the size of the ring pops I'd strutted around wearing as a child.

We were already bound together, but Zyon was making it official, so there could be no questioning our relationship. Forgetting my nerves and all the eyes focused on us, I pushed past the ring and dropped to my knees in front of Zyon.

"Yes!" I blinked back tears, knowing Kelsey would kill me if I ruined my makeup by crying. "I love you too, Zyon. I want to spend the rest of my life with you."

Zyon pulled me into his arms and stood. He twirled me around before setting me on my feet and sliding the ring on my finger. Turning to the crowd, he grinned and shouted, "She said yes!"

The room erupted into cheers, whistles, and more than a few sobs. Trumpets blared, and a guard bellowed above the crowd's noise. "Zyon Timotei Milosovici, Crown Prince of the Vampire Kingdom and his fiancé, our future princess, Journee Elsher."

Looping my arm through his, Zyon proudly led me down the staircase toward the throng waiting to congratulate us.

I CLUNG to Zyon's arms as vampire after vampire came to congratulate us. There were a few nasty looks directed my way, but for the most part, the vampires went out of their way to make me feel welcomed into their world.

As Zyon chatted with several businessmen, I took in the opulent ballroom. Rather than a floor of marble and a gold ceiling, the floor was made of gold leaf, and the walls were white marble. Golden veins ran through the marble and glittered in the romantic lighting of the room.

The ceiling was made of intricately carved wood with a gold dust patina. It was breathtaking and a reminder I was way out of my depth.

I was a clerk in a clothing store where I waited on the type of women who fought over invitations for parties like this. Yet there I was, strolling into the royal ballroom as though I had every right to be there.

"Close your mouth. You're gonna catch flies," Turik whispered from where he stood guard behind me.

"I can't help it!" I whispered back. "We hold our parties in barns where I come from!"

"There is nothing wrong with that." Turik gave me a sincere smile. "I've been to many barn parties, and I would rather be there surrounded by friends and enjoying a potluck dinner than attending any of these perfectly orchestrated shows."

"Then why are you here? Are you forced to work for the queen?"

"Of course not." Turik chuckled. "We all choose to be here in the queen's service. When you're an old vampire, you find it hard to keep up with changing times. It's easier to stay in the palace, where things remain the same. But I'd give my right arm for a bowl of real, homemade potato salad."

My stomach rumbled. "My mom makes the best potato salad."

A sad wave of homesickness washed through me. I

missed my parents. Things had become so chaotic I hadn't had a chance to even call them.

Now I was bound to a vampire, and our engagement had just been announced to the world... and I hadn't even told them.

Getting engaged felt like the type of thing you were supposed to share with your parents in person. When we got back to our room this evening, I'd tell Zyon I needed to make a trip home to visit my parents. Maybe he'd even come with me.

A couple of hours later, we stood on the marble porch that opened out into the gardens. Fairy lights twinkled in the trees and perfectly trimmed bushes.

It had begun to rain. Not a heavy downpour, but a light sprinkling that added to the soundtrack of the evening. Standing beneath the balcony overhead, we were able to stay dry while spending time with our friends.

Zyon was beaming proudly at my side, and that was all that mattered to me.

One face was conspicuously missing. Ella still hadn't made an appearance.

Leaning into Zyon's embrace, I whispered, "Where's Ella? Did she get so mad she packed up and left?"

"I hope so, for her sake," Zyon snarled. "You distracted me yesterday, but I'm still considering snapping her neck when I see her. She'd be wise to get far away from me and stay there."

She didn't seem like the type to give up when she wanted something.

"Should we send someone to check on her?" An icy chill traveled down my spine, and a warning began to blare inside my skull.

Something wasn't right. I didn't know how I knew... but I knew. Danger lurked nearby.

A scream and a crash came from overhead.

Zyon jerked me into the safety of his arms as something fell from the balcony above and slammed into the lanai with a sickening crunch.

Chaos erupted as men swore and women screamed.

But for me, the world had frozen as I stared into the lifeless eyes of the woman who lay like a broken doll on the cold, wet marble.

Ella Wessex.

Pushing out of Zyon's arms, I stumbled toward Ella as though I were drawn to her by an invisible force. An unfamiliar male vampire rushed forward, pressing his fingers to her neck and checking for a pulse he wouldn't find.

The queen pushed through the row of guards who'd moved to block the guests from viewing Ella's broken body and stood next to me.

"Is she—" the queen started.

The man stood, his knees wet with a mix of rain and blood. "She's dead."

The queen leaned in close to my ear and whispered low enough that only I could hear her words. "When I said you could throw some girls over the balcony, I didn't think you would take me literally."

Hiccups racked my body, causing my chest to heave, and my entire body grew slick with sweat.

"Relax. You're safe." The queen patted my hand, even as Zyon's arms circled my body.

"What killed her?" Nathan asked from behind us. "It wasn't the fall. At this distance, she might've broken some things, but it wouldn't have been fatal."

"Agreed." Zyon tried to angle his body so that he protected me from most of the rain. "But there are no signs of other injuries. It appears she fell over the balcony."

Unable to look away, I stared into Ella's glassy eyes. The last time I'd seen those eyes, they'd been filled with so much hatred. She'd sworn she would kill me, and I truly believed she meant it. But I still wouldn't have wished her dead.

Zyon was right. Ella's body appeared uninjured. Other than three thin cuts along her cheek.

How strange.

What were the odds that she would have three cuts on the same cheek, in exactly the same place as the ones her nails had sliced into mine less than twenty-four hours ago?

The cuts were exactly the same.

No, no, no.

I tried to breathe, but my lungs refused to expand.

He was here.

It made no sense! Why would he kill her?

Because he was delusional and believed I belonged to him. She'd threatened me and paid for it with her life.

That meant Abner had been nearby. Watching and listening.

Was he watching us now?

"There's something in her hand," Kelsey whispered, pointing toward Ella's tightly clenched fist.

In the human world, police would've been called and evidence bags used. Things worked differently in the vampire world. The man who'd checked for Ella's pulse leaned down and pried her fingers from around a black object.

It fell from her hand and into a puddle of bloody rainwater.

Light from the ballroom lit the figurine of a tiny black cat.

The exact same figurine I'd been given as a child and had been on display in my apartment.

Any doubts I had vanished. Abner had killed Ella, and he wanted me to know he'd done it for me.

I began to sob, and my legs collapsed beneath me as my terror consumed me.

ZYON CAUGHT me before I hit the ground and cradled me in his arms. Without saying a word to anyone, he blurred through the castle, taking me to the safety of our room.

The moment the bedroom door locked behind us, I

wailed, letting out the anger that was turning into a living thing inside me.

Why wouldn't he leave me alone? Abner had taken so much from me, and yet he continued to terrorize my life from the shadows.

Tonight should've been one of the happiest nights of my life, and thanks to his actions, it would forever be marred with the gruesome memory of Ella's broken body.

She wasn't a great person or even someone I liked, but she didn't deserve to be murdered.

Thanks to my presence in the castle, she'd been put squarely in the crosshairs of my psychopathic stalker.

"It's my fault she's dead," I choked out between sobs.

"It's not." Zyon grabbed my jaw, forcing my head up to look at him. "We don't know why she died. I don't know how you've gotten it into your head that this is your fault, but it's not."

"Abner killed her, and it's because of me!" His face was a blur through my tears, but I heard the way his breath caught at my words.

"Journee, there were no signs of a fight or a struggle on her body. Why would you think Abner was responsible for this?"

"Didn't you see the scratches? They were exact matches to the scratches she sliced into my cheek yesterday." I swiped at the tears streaming down my face.

Zyon hadn't made the connection, and I could see the wheels in his mind begin to turn. Still, he tried to comfort me. "That's just a coincidence."

"And the cat?"

Zyon shrugged. "What about it? It was probably some trinket Ella carried for luck."

"No, it's not. It's exactly the same figurine as the one I had in my apartment. I think it *is* mine. It's the same little cat I was constantly adjusting because it would be facing the wrong way on the shelf. I always thought I must have bumped the shelf to make it shift positions, but now I think Abner was moving it as some twisted way of letting me know he'd been there."

"Are you sure?" Zyon spoke through clenched teeth, an ominous glow burning in his eyes.

Instead of answering, I covered my face with my hands and burst into fresh tears.

"Journee, listen to me. Even if Abner did this to avenge you or as a warning, it isn't your fault! Ella threatened you —she hurt you. Frick, I would've killed her yesterday if you hadn't stopped me."

I couldn't respond, and simply curled into a tight ball in the middle of his bed.

Zyon crawled onto the bed, curving his body around mine and tucking me against him. "Shhh. Don't cry, Tumbleweed. Neither of them are worth your tears."

"I've made a mess of both of our lives. You would've been better off if you'd never met me." My voice broke, and I pressed my knuckles against my mouth to keep from screaming at the unfairness of it all.

"You couldn't be more wrong." Zyon's snarl vibrated through me, turning my bones to jelly. "I've lived many human lifetimes. This is the only time I remember being happy. You are the best thing to ever happen to me. My treasure from the fates."

We lay in silence for several minutes before I could speak. "There's something else, Zyon. Someone in the castle knows I'm a Hunter. Or at least they suspect it."

His body went rigid. "What makes you think that?"

I relayed what had happened after I left the queen's chambers. When I finished, I held my breath. Would this be the moment he decided I was too much work? That I had brought trouble to the castle?

"What did she look like?"

I relayed what I could remember. Zyon pulled his phone from his pocket to relay the information to the guards.

"How did she know what I am, Zyon?"

He paused his typing to stare into my eyes. "Because she was a Hunter. That means there are two Hunters lurking around the castle."

"I can't figure it out. If she is helping Abner with a plan to abduct me, why would she tell me to stay with you?"

Zyon was quiet.

"Zyon?" I prompted.

"Let it go. Please let it go," he pleaded. His thumb brushed my lips.

"I can't. I need to know."

"Because she believes at some point you won't be able to fight against the Hunter's instincts to kill. And when that happens, if you are near me and my grandmother, you'd have a better shot at killing the royal family than the Hunters have had for centuries."

Flattening my palms against his chest, I tried to push away. But Zyon held me tight, refusing to release me.

"You have to let me go before I hurt someone!"

Still, Zyon held me tight, refusing to let me leave.

"Zyon! What if I kill you while you're sleeping? I could never live with myself if I hurt you!" Tears streamed down my cheeks.

He kissed my tears away. "I'm not afraid of you, little mate."

"But I am," I whispered, voice breaking. "I don't want to be a Hunter. I don't want to kill."

"It will all work out." Zyon rubbed my back, trying to soothe me so I could sleep.

He loved me, but he hadn't assured me that I wouldn't kill.

Because he couldn't.

"The depths to which your idiocy sinks will never cease to amaze me." Mari flopped onto the couch, kicking her feet up on the table and chugging half her beer.

The manliness of her behavior was disgusting, and I found myself once again thankful she wasn't my betrothed. I would have needed an entire keg of alcohol to bed that woman.

With Journee, I'd never need to drink. It would be an insult to dull my senses before making love to her. And I'd need full control of my body to ensure my knives didn't cut too deep or permanently injure her during our couplings.

"Loverboy! Are you listening?" Mari threw an expired men's magazine at my head. "This is a huge day for Hunters. We should be celebrating, but instead, you're sulking like a petulant toddler."

I bit my tongue to keep from losing my temper with her. She held a higher rank, and I needed her to believe I was following her orders. "It is hard to celebrate when my betrothed just became engaged to a bloodsucking demon."

"It's beyond perfect. I tested her spark today, and it was glowing but hadn't fully awoken. She's going to fully spark anytime and will slaughter the prince and those closest to him. It will be the biggest blow the Hunters have ever dealt the vampiric kingdom." Mari grinned and took another long drink from her beer. "You'll just have to be willing to accept sloppy seconds."

"I will always accept what is best for the Hunters," I ground out through clenched teeth.

"Good. Because I learned the details of her wedding date. If she hasn't sparked by then, I want the team stationed near the castle. There hasn't been a royal wedding in three centuries, so everyone who's anyone will be in attendance. If we find an opening, we will attack. Gather the rest of the Hunters and prepare them." Grabbing the remote, she flipped on the TV.

Clearly, I was dismissed.

Standing, I made my way to my chambers. I punched the wall, rage roiling like lava in my blood. He'd proposed, and she'd accepted.

Journee had promised herself to someone else.

Another man's ring had been placed on her finger.

How could she love me when she continued to steal the moments that should be special for us?

I knew she was terrified, trapped in a castle filled with vampires, but how far would she be willing to go to stay on the prince's good side? Would she say 'I do?'

I'd tolerated her teasing and her desire to prolong our union, knowing it would add to the pleasure we'd experience when we finally consummated our love. But I refused to allow her to give the abomination a wedding night with her.

I prayed she was resisting his advances and staying pure for me, but at this point, the prince may have grown weary of waiting. I'd accepted that he may have already taken what he wanted.

Zyon would die for touching her, and Journee would spend years groveling to make up for allowing him to find pleasure in her body. But with time, we'd heal, and she'd come to understand the level of heartache her impulsive decisions had inflicted on me.

But I drew the line at her becoming his wife, even if the vows were a farce.

Tonight, she'd allowed him to slip that gaudy ring on her finger, and although it had cut like a knife to the heart, I'd still put aside my hurt to show my love. I'd delivered the body of her would-be killer at Journee's feet.

Ella had been an easy kill, thanks to the vampire toxin we'd finally perfected. It had been risky to take the time to carve the lines in Ella's cheek and to tuck the figurine into her hand, but it had been worth it.

Journee had instantly recognized the gift for what it was and had been rendered speechless. When her knees buckled, I knew I'd marked her heart in a way the prince could never dream of.

He'd been too weak to take care of the bratty vampiress

who'd terrorized Journee. Now Journee would know I was the only man willing to risk everything to protect her.

Time was ticking.

Grabbing a notepad, I began to prepare for the reunion with my girl.

CHAPTER 18

journee

The rest of the week was quiet. With our engagement announced, Zyon and I were not required to attend any of the social events going on in the castle.

Turik guided me from my final fitting with Jamis back to Zyon's room. We passed a set of windows, and my heart lurched at the crowd milling on the castle lawn. I'd thought most of the castle's guests, especially the females, would have returned home. But instead, even more visitors had flooded the castle grounds.

"I can't believe so many people stayed after what happened to Ella."

Turik patted my shoulder, reminding me of how my father would do the same when I struggled with my homework. "Are you kidding? I suspect every vampire in the kingdom is dying to be here right now. This is the juiciest gossip to happen in centuries."

"The prince's wedding? The fact I'm human? Or Ella's death?"

Turik chuckled. "All three! This is better than any reality TV show they could be watching at home."

Zyon must have heard our voices in the hall because he leaned against the bedroom doorway, his eyes watching us as we made our way down the hall.

"This is where I leave you, Miss Journee. But I assure you, you couldn't be in better hands." He winked, then turned on his heel and blurred away.

Going up on my tiptoes, I kissed Zyon's cheek and stumbled into the room, collapsing face-first onto the bed.

"Who knew standing still was so exhausting?" My words were muffled by the silky blankets.

Zyon's husky laugh sent a wave of heat rippling through me, but I was too tired to do anything about it.

"My poor little princess," Zyon cooed, leaning down to tickle my sides.

Princess.

I was going to make a terrible princess. Heck, when I dropped an ice cube on the floor, I still kicked it under the fridge rather than picking it up like an adult. There was no way I was prepared to have more responsibility.

"I spoke with Nathan earlier, and he told me several hundred more vampires will arrive for the ceremony tonight."

Groaning, I rolled to my back and stared at the ceiling. "Hundreds? Are you sure we can't just have a small, intimate ceremony?"

Zyon sat down next to me and brushed my lips with a featherlight kiss. "I know this is asking a lot, Tumbleweed.

This probably isn't anything like the wedding you hoped for, but after our wedding, we will be free to do whatever you want. If you want to disappear to an island and not talk to anyone for the next decade, I'll make it happen."

Tapping my chin, I gave him a sly look. "Recently, I'd considered becoming a coconut farmer."

"Oh, really? Well, if that's what your heart desires, consider it done." Zyon shifted to settle his body over mine.

His weight pressed me into the mattress, and his lips captured my mouth in a toe-curling kiss. When he pulled away, he asked, "Have you given any thought to what you would like our future to be? Or where in this vast world would you like to call home?"

His kiss had turned my brain to mush, and he wanted me to discuss life plans? I couldn't even remember how to spell my name.

I ran my fingers through his hair, loving the fall of the silken strands between my fingers. "Where's your favorite place? That's where I want to go."

He opened his mouth to answer, but I pressed a finger to his lips.

"Don't tell me! I want you to surprise me."

Zyon lifted an eyebrow. "I thought you didn't like surprises?"

"I absolutely hate them! But this will be an adventure. But first, I want to visit my parents. Would you be willing to come with me?"

"You don't even need to ask." Zyon's expression softened. "Are you sure you don't want to invite them tonight?"

I shook my head. "I don't think my parents have ever left my tiny hometown. Being in a castle surrounded by vampires probably wouldn't make them very comfortable. Plus, I want to talk to them in person, not over the phone."

"Journee," Zyon hesitated. "You know that for you to be a Hunter, at least one of your parents would have to be a Hunter too, right?"

I played with the button on his dress shirt. "I know, but it doesn't make sense. My parents are farmers. The only knife my mom handles is the one she uses to slice vegetables. I'm telling you, she couldn't slice into a living creature. She started sobbing when Dad was going to kill one of the extra roosters for us to eat. My mother ended up keeping it as her pet." I giggled at the memory. "That rooster would sit in her lap in the evenings, and she would pet him while reading the newspaper."

"I look forward to meeting your mother." Zyon kissed the tip of my nose. "If your mother isn't a Hunter, then it has to be your dad."

I sighed. "That makes even less sense! My dad would give his neighbor the shirt off his back. Not to mention he would lack the speed needed to take on a vampire. I've never seen my dad even run! If the house was on fire, my dad would still walk to put it out. That man is never in a hurry."

Zyon opened his mouth but changed his mind and closed it.

"If they were Hunters, wouldn't they have warned me? What kind of parent would have just let their kid go out into the world where they might awaken at any time and start massacring vampires?"

"I hate to ask this, but could you be adopted? Maybe they don't know what you are because they aren't your birth parents." Zyon's voice was gentle, probably realizing it was something I didn't want to think about.

"I suppose it's possible, but I look just like my parents." I chewed on my lip.

"Lots of people think adopted families look similar. Perhaps that's the case with your family?"

"Maybe. I'd like to talk to them about it, but if they don't know about Hunters, it's probably safer for them to be kept in the dark."

Zyon rolled us over so that I rested on his chest while he hugged me close. "We'll figure it out. First, let's survive our wedding. Then we can figure out the rest of our lives."

Closing my eyes, I listened to the reassuring sound of his heartbeat.

Zyon rubbed slow circles on my back. "Everything will work out. You have nothing to worry about, my love."

I wanted to believe him, but it was hard. Nothing had gone smoothly the past week. We still hadn't been able to prove whether Ella had been murdered or if her death was an accident.

I knew in my heart Abner was responsible. Which meant he was still out there, watching and waiting. Maybe when he found out I was married, it would break his illusion that we were betrothed.

I was going to cling to that hope.

I jumped at the knock on the door, and Zyon chuckled.

"I would guess that's your wedding team. Are you ready to become Mrs. Milosovici?"

I kissed him on the lips. "I've never been more ready!"

We moved to open the door, revealing a grinning Kelsey, Jamis, and six other ladies. They each carried multiple bags stuffed full of what I presumed were things needed to get me presentable to walk down the aisle.

Kelsey and Jamis linked arms with me and dragged me from Zyon's room.

"Come on. The queen has given us a room closer to the throne room where we can get you ready!"

Jamis laughed. "Which is a good thing since you suck in heels, and this will make your walk to the ceremony far shorter."

He snapped his fingers. "But we don't have all day! Let's get a move on, ladies."

Blowing a kiss over my shoulder at my sexy fiancé, I allowed myself to be led away. It wouldn't be much longer until I could be alone with Zyon and away from the interruptions of the world.

TAKING A DEEP BREATH, I straightened my spine and strode toward the throne room doors. As I neared, the door opened, revealing an enchanted world of cascading crimson-red roses.

The moment my toe touched the rose-strewn aisle that led toward the throne, music began to play. Without making a sound, the wedding guests rose, turning to watch me make my way to my waiting groom.

Unlike a human wedding where the guests avoided wearing black, all the attendees wore perfectly tailored black suits and elegant black evening gowns.

The contrast of the gold ceiling and walls of the throne room, with the blood-red roses and inky-black attire, made for a wedding far more beautiful than anything I could've dreamed up.

My dress had been created in a ruby-red silk so soft it was like petals against my skin. Instead of the long train I'd assumed would be required for a royal wedding, Jamis had sculpted a gown fit for a Greek goddess.

I'd felt guilty about pushing the wedding planning off onto the castle's team of party planners. But the idea of trying to plan a magazine-worthy wedding in a matter of days was a monumental task that I didn't have the skills to tackle. It had been a relief to let the experts handle it.

There was also the fear I'd turn into a bridezilla who got stressed out and started murdering vampires. I preferred the safety of Zyon's room... and arms.

Roaming the castle to meet with a list of wedding

vendors—all of whom would be complete strangers to me —sounded like trouble waiting to happen.

It was for the best that I limited the time I spent around the vampires, at least until I knew what was going on with me and how I could control it.

I still worried I'd accidentally hurt Zyon, but he laughed away my concerns and assured me he'd probably enjoy it.

In the past couple of days, I hadn't experienced any more episodes where I wanted to kill someone, but I'd also been far more fatigued than usual.

As I walked down the aisle toward my soulmate, my limbs felt heavy, as though they were full of lead.

Just a few more hours.

Zyon's eyes watched me, adoration, and hunger on his face.

In a few minutes, he would be my husband, and I'd be his wife.

The thought sent a thrill through me, and I forced myself not to walk faster, no matter how eager I was to be at his side.

CHAPTER 19

journee

Halfway down the aisle, I felt the familiar bubbling in my chest that signified a bout of hiccups.

Not now, please, I pleaded with my body.

The throne room was huge on a medieval scale, but the room was packed with vampires. They surrounded me and watched my every step.

I was a mouse wandering through a den of vipers.

DANGER.

I kept a frozen smile on my face to hide my wince of pain from the clanging warning system sounding in my mind.

VAMPIRES.

Locking eyes with Zyon, I tried to let my anxiety fade and focus instead on how much I wanted to be his wife.

This was not the time or place to have a freakout. I could already imagine the headlines. Zyon's eyes tightened with worry, and he took a step toward me.

My legs wobbled, and dizziness washed through me.

An arm looped through mine, steadying me. With effort, I focused on the vampire next to me.

Turik gave me a reassuring smile and whispered, "I know humans have a tradition of fathers walking their daughters down the aisle. Would you allow me to escort you to the prince?"

Turik was allowing me to save my pride by not mentioning how I was two seconds from face-planting in the aisle. He'd broken royal protocol by stepping in, and I wondered how much trouble he'd just brought down on his head.

I'd fight the queen over this if I had to. Relieved, I clung to him like he was a float and I was drowning. "Thank you, Turik."

He bowed his head and began to guide me forward. His red uniform and golden armor matched my dress beautifully. With Turik supporting most of my weight, we glided closer to my groom.

DANGER.

My heart thudded against my chest, each beat slower than the last. What was wrong with me? Was I having a panic attack?

DANGER. DANGER. DANGER.

I couldn't think over the warning pounding against my skull.

My body seemed to be moving through quicksand, and I was becoming increasingly lethargic with each step I took.

PROTECT.

That was new. Who was I supposed to protect?

A shiver trailed down my spine, and my chest burned like someone was holding a branding iron to it.

VAMPIRES.

I wasn't in danger from the vampires.

They were the ones in danger, and they didn't even know it.

I met Zyon's wide eyes, and I knew who I needed to protect.

Releasing Turik's arm, I summoned every last bit of my waning energy I could muster and blurred forward.

Time slowed as I ran until I could see the darts moving through the air around me. They were aimed at the prince and the queen, who stood ready to officiate the wedding.

"No!" I screamed. Pushing myself harder and ignoring the way my heart was struggling to find a steady rhythm, I blurred ahead of the needle-sharp weapons.

Reaching the end of the aisle, I grabbed a shield from a guard standing at attention. I spun around, and with trembling arms, lifted the heavy shield in front of me.

In a whoosh, time returned to normal. The momentum I'd built up now turned on me, throwing my body backward.

The ping of metal hitting metal was music to my ears, even as I slammed into Zyon and the queen and heard something in my body snap.

I lay on top of the royal family, unable to move even a pinky.

The queen shoved me off her. "What is wrong with you?"

Zyon hurried to gather me in his arms. "Are you okay? Why did you—"

He stopped and looked down. We both stared in horror at the needle buried in his knee.

"Isn't that ironic? Journee just drained her spark to save your life, and in your hurry to save her, you kneeled down on one of our darts." The woman's laughter lacked humor and was cold as ice.

"Who are you?" the queen demanded of the wedding crasher.

"I'm Mari, current Head Huntress of the Hunter Guild."

"*You,*" I croaked.

"Yes, I'm the one who snuck in to see how close you were to sparking. We were going to let you handle this mission on your own, but having so many of our targets trapped in one room was too good of an opportunity to pass up."

She whistled, and several Hunters stepped to block the entrances. They held weapons that reminded me of a bow, except it was metal and lined with rows upon rows of those tiny needles.

Mari waggled a finger at the gathered vampires. "I'd suggest everyone take a seat. Those weapons are automatic and will spray hundreds of darts within seconds. A single dart carries enough toxin to kill three vampires. One wrong move, and we will spray the entire room."

And one of those darts had buried itself in Zyon's skin. He sagged against the wall next to me, sweat beading his brow.

I wanted to scream or to throw myself at this evil woman, but I couldn't. Because I was dying. My heartbeat was erratic and sluggish, and my breathing came in shallow, rasping breaths.

Mari squatted down next to me, clicking her tongue in disappointment. "I had high hopes for you. But instead of letting your spark activate properly, you drained it to save these filthy demons. Since you struggle to understand loyalties, it's better for you to die now than to become an issue later."

"Antidote?" I whispered.

"Seriously? You're dying, and you still want to help the fangers?" Mari shook her head in disgust. "I'll let you in on a secret. There is an antidote, but it's the one thing no vampire can ever get their hands on. Which is why this is the perfect weapon against them."

A window overhead exploded, raining shards of glass down on us. Zyon leaned over me, protecting me even as he struggled to breathe, and his muscles jerked violently as the toxin spread through his bloodstream.

"Mari! What is going on?" Abner's bellow echoed around the expansive throne room. "This was not the plan!"

Great. Now that he'd arrived, it was a real party. Not.

Mari rested her hands on her hips and smirked up at my stalker, who leaned over the balcony above us. "Glad you could join us, Abner. This was always the plan. We just didn't tell you because you've developed a bad habit of going rogue."

"You tricked me? How dare you try to make a fool of me!" he roared, disappearing from the balcony and appearing a few feet away from us.

"Me make a fool of you?" Mari scoffed. "You do that all on your own. Look at you! You've become obsessed with Journee, and you've let it affect your decisions."

"Journee is valuable!" he snarled. "She's twice the Huntress you could ever hope to be."

Mari waved toward me. "If that was the case, why did she burn herself out to save a demon? She's as foolish as you."

"You don't know what you're talking about!" Abner's face turned a mottled red as he spat the words in her face. "She did what she had to do to survive being held by the prince!"

"You are an embarrassment to the guild and blind to reality." Mari rolled her eyes and turned to me. "The vampire prince is dying. He can't protect you—not that you'll need it since your body is already shutting down. Tell this imbecile the truth."

My vision was darkening, but I moved my head enough to meet Abner's hopeful gaze.

"I love Zyon with every fiber of my being." I fought to catch my breath. "I'd rather die at his side than live a single day by your side."

Abner's furious scream was music to my ears.

I might be dying, but he didn't get what he wanted, and that made me incredibly happy.

"Now sit down over there." Mari motioned toward a far wall. "We can't have you getting in our way."

I watched through cracked eyelids as the Hunters corralled the vampires into groups. They kept enough weapons aimed at each group to ensure no one tried to be a hero.

Zyon's body pressed behind me, his hand finding mine, and his cool fingers wrapped around mine. A thin trickle of dark blood trailed trickled from a cut on his arm.

I wished I could lick him and heal it.

"...the one thing no vampire can ever get their hands on..." Mari's words drifted through my foggy mind.

Blood.

Hunter blood.

Could that be the antidote?

"Zy...on."

There was a pause before he responded. "Hm?"

"My blood... cure... bite me." It took immense effort to speak. "Don't... argue."

Zyon's fangs sliced into the nape of my neck. Our position made it impossible for the Hunters to see what he was doing.

With each pull of my blood, his breathing grew steadier. It would take time for him to heal, but as my heart fluttered and stopped, I smiled, knowing he would live.

"No, you don't," Zyon's soft whisper came from a thousand miles away.

Comforting warmth stroked across my skin and seeped

into my body. It was like receiving a hundred hugs at the same time.

"You can't leave me, Irenvyth."

My heart fluttered, skipped, then gave a soft *thump*.

Heat surged through my chest, and my heart responded with a thump.

Keeping a steady rhythm, the heat surged into me over and over. With each pulse, my heart responded with a *thump* until my heart remembered how to beat and began to thud against my rib cage.

"Zyon?"

"Shhh, Tumbleweed. We don't want them to notice us." Zyon's lips tickled the back of my neck.

"How?"

"Your blood is burning through the toxin in my body, but I'm still too weak to shift. The shadows answered my call. They refused to let your heart stop."

Cracking my eyes open, I watched the shadows rolling over my limp arm. They stayed close to the floor to avoid being noticed.

I looked around at the terrified vampires cowering as the Hunters taunted them over who would die first. The queen had been shoved to the floor, and Mari sat on the throne, twirling the queen's crown on her finger.

Rage simmered in my gut, and the spark Mari claimed I'd drained flickered in my chest.

If the shadows could kickstart my heart... would they be able to do the same to my Hunter abilities?

I didn't even have to ask. The shadows curled around

my body and sank beneath my skin. My chest began to glow as the shadows blew on the dying embers of my spark.

As the embers turned to a blaze, a new level of power spread through my veins.

Casting my eyes around the room, I made a plan.

It would work, or we'd all die… but I'd make sure I took the Hunters down with us.

CHAPTER
20

journee

"**D**on't do it," Zyon hissed.

"You don't know what I'm going to do," I whispered, keeping my lips as still as possible in case anyone was looking my way.

"I can feel the energy crackling across your skin, and your Hunter scent is growing stronger. You're going to try and be a hero. Run fast, and don't look back. Save yourself." His command was laced with a plea. "I can't watch you die again."

"Then you should probably close your eyes in case things go south." I flexed my fingers, testing my strength. "Because I have a vampire soulmate to save and a crown to take back."

One by one, I tested every muscle in my body. I'd only get one shot at this.

"Bax!" Mari called to one of the Hunters. "I think we should start with the queen. Let all her loyal subjects see how helpless even the most powerful vampires are against

Hunters. It's a shame the abomination took himself out so early."

"Get on your knees." Bax kicked the queen hard enough to crack her ribs.

Without whimpering or showing any sign of the pain she had to be in, the queen rose to her knees. She kept her back straight and her head lifted.

She was regal as frick, and a seed of respect bloomed in my chest.

I counted the Hunters spread around the room. There were eight, not counting Abner and Mari. Neither Abner nor Mari held one of the dart guns, but that didn't mean they were unarmed.

With no time to waste, I reached for the spark glowing in my chest and called every bit of Hunter energy I could to me. Surging to my feet, I flickered across the room, seeming to be more energy than flesh.

I slammed into Bax, the Hunter holding the weapon to the queen's head. Punching my arm forward, I'd intended to hit his chest, but my arm punched straight through, like a hot knife through butter.

It was disgusting, but I didn't have time to dwell on it as I ricocheted around the room, taking out one Hunter after another.

I was down to Abner, Mari, and the Hunter guarding Abner when I heard a roar of rage. Spinning around, I found a bolt of energy crackling from Mari straight toward me.

There was no way to dodge something moving faster

than me, so I braced for the impact. That's when Turik came into focus as he threw himself between the blast and me.

He must have guessed her intentions and moved to block it before she'd even thrown the deadly blast.

"No!" I screamed, rushing toward him but unable to get to him before the blast of energy burned through his chest.

White-hot rage and adrenaline were a powerful cocktail, and before his body had even hit the ground, I was holding Mari by her neck.

Energy surged and popped around me, fed by my fury.

"He was my friend!" I snarled in her face.

"Oops. Sorry." Mari curled her lip. "He was a fanged demon, and his death makes the world a better place."

"That's where you're wrong." My fingers tightened around her neck. "But your death certainly will."

Instead of crushing her throat and being done with it, I wanted her to experience the same fear the vampires had felt at her cruelty.

Sending my energy surging through her, I was careful to not kill her. I was focused on finding her spark. Once my magic had connected to hers, I pulled the Hunter's energy from her body.

I didn't stop until her spark was drained, and she lay at my feet. Powerless and slowly dying as her drained body began to shut down.

Turning, I searched for Abner and the only Hunter I hadn't yet killed. They'd disappeared. I cursed out loud, angry they'd escaped my wrath... for now.

The large throne room doors rattled. They had been

barricaded by the Hunters, but something, or someone, wanted in. We didn't have to wait long to find out who. With the forced of an explosion, the doors were blasted open. An ominous smoke rolled into the room.

Squinting, I prepared for another attack as two leather-clad figures emerged from the haze. Small beams of light filtered through the dust and smoke and glinted off the swords and knives strapped to newcomers' bodies.

The queen gasped, and I was surprised to find her composure had slipped, and for the first time during this entire fiasco, she looked terrified.

"Who are they?" I hissed, unable to make out the faces thanks to their masks.

"They are the Savages." Her words were barely audible. "The most powerful family of Hunters to walk this earth."

Well, crap.

Just when I thought we were going to live through this, I found out we were going to die.

Moving to stand between the queen and the Hunters, I prepared for one last fight.

The pair of Hunters stopped a few feet from me and slowly reached up to pull the masks from their faces.

I inhaled sharply. "Mom? Dad?"

"WHAT ARE YOU DOING HERE?" I gaped at them, my mind unable to make sense of their sudden appearance.

Maybe I had died, and this was a dream.

My dad stepped forward and pulled me into the kind of bear hug only a dad could give. "We could ask you the same thing, Sprout. You're supposed to be working at a clothing store in the city. So how is it that we come for a visit to find you getting married to the vampire Crown Prince?"

Mom stepped forward and began checking me for injuries. "You look thin, honey. Have you been eating enough?"

My parents were dressed in leather, and every vampire in the room was frozen in a stupefied terror, but here my mom was worrying if I'd remembered to eat.

Her fingers brushed against the back of my neck, and I winced.

"You're hurt!" She brushed my hair away from my neck, displaying the vampire bite mark for the world to see. "Oh, my."

Audible gasps rippled through the room. I stepped from my dad's embrace and made my way to stand in front of the queen, who still kneeled on the ground.

"Hunter blood is the antidote to the toxin-filled darts. Zyon fed from me to heal himself." I hesitated. "But this is not the first time I shared my blood with him. I'm not ashamed of being able to provide something my soulmate needs. And frankly, it is none of anyone's business what we do behind closed doors."

"They don't want to know. Some things can't be unseen," Nathan mumbled a little too loudly.

Ignoring Nathan, I offered my hand to the queen and helped her stand.

I held out the crown I still had in my hand. "This belongs to you. I'm not sure where we stand now, and I can understand if you don't want a Hunter in the castle—"

The queen threw her arms around my neck and hugged me tight. "Thank you."

I patted her back, unsure what I was supposed to do.

"Grandmother, you should probably release her before Journee's parents release the knives they have aimed at you."

Zyon's hands grabbed my waist and turned me around to face him.

Tilting my head back, I stared up at my gorgeous mate. "Do you still want me?"

"Just because your last name is Savage instead of Elsher doesn't change the fact I'm going to make you my wife. We'll just have to plan a new wedding."

"One that we're invited to!" my dad added, walking to us and offering his hand to Zyon. "Welcome to the family. We're retired, by the way. Just dusted off the gear when we heard rumors of an impending attack and thought y'all might need help."

Zyon clasped my father's hand, and hope burst through me that maybe this could start something new between Hunters and vampires.

My eyes trailed across the traumatized faces of the

vampires who'd slowly begun to trickle from the room and the prone body of the guard who'd been my friend.

"I won't let them get away with this. It's time the guild was shut down," I snarled, static electricity crackling and popping around me.

"That shouldn't be too hard to do since you killed the head Huntress and took her power." My mom stood from where she'd been crouched over Mari's body, her eyes glowing a brilliant green. "Which makes you the new leader of the guild."

My stomach fell to the floor before lurching up into my throat.

"What?" I squeaked.

"Rules are rules, Sprout." My dad chuckled. "You're the head Huntress, whether you like it or not."

I looked around at the faces of the people I wanted to protect. "Then I think it's time for the Hunters to become the Hunted."

ABOUT DARCI R. ACULA

Darci R. Acula is Sedona Ashe's not-so-secret pen name. Sedona's books tend to focus on Reverse Harem relationships, while Darci's books feature only MF relationships.

Darci (aka Sedona) doesn't reserve her sarcasm for her books; her poor husband can tell you that her wit, humor, and snarky attitude are just part of her daily life. While she loves writing paranormal shifter reverse harem novels, she's a sucker for true love, twisted situations, and wacky humor.

Darci lives in a small town at the base of the Great Smoky Mountains in Tennessee. She and her husband share their home with their three children, adorable pup, five cats, pet arctic fox, chickens, several crazy turkeys, two chubby frogs, and over a hundred other reptiles. When she isn't working, she enjoys getting away from the computer to hike, free dive, travel, study languages, and capture images of places and animals through her photography. Darci has a crazy goal of writing a million words in a year, and spending six months exploring Indonesia.

You can find more information about the author and her books here:

www.authorsedonaashe.com
www.instagram.com/sedonaashe
www.facebook.com/sedonaashe

www.ingramcontent.com/pod-product-compliance
Lightning Source LLC
Chambersburg PA
CBHW020434180626
46812CB00003B/1225